LIFE WITHOUT DEATH

Contents

Circumstances Surrounding
My Birth

MY MOTHER FIRST encountered the word "salient" in the fiction section of one of her magazines and tried it out on my father during a serving of her legendary braised lamb shanks. At the time, Dad was having problems with a co-worker at the carpentry shop. Luckily, as my mother explained, these problems were not "salient," and in fact the next day the co-worker was fired, my father's adoration of my mother increased, and the word "salient" became central to their marriage.

Part of that marriage consisted of two hours in the afternoon when my mother set out to learn everything. She did this at the local library or in the kitchen of Stella Davenport, who had a B.A. in English literature, and was putting it to use raising twins. From these visits she learned that Canadians were more salient than they were a decade earlier, Americans were salient only if they lived in New York. The British were salient, especially Keats, who was hugely salient, and the French were salient without even trying.

One night it happened that my parents went to a party where they were introduced to a large, laughing man who gripped my father's hand with the easy confidence of a man who flies airplanes for a living. "Thomas Selwyn Brittan," he said. "Call me Tommy." He was in fact an airline pilot. My father, unable to take his eyes off my mother, paid no attention to the man. "Bill," he said weakly, shifting to one side to get a better view of his wife. "Bill Withers."

A large part of that evening was spent discussing how Mr. Thomas Selwyn Brittan had once landed a crippled airliner in a Saskatchewan cornfield without spilling the passengers' drinks. My father leaned against a wall staring at my mother, and barely heard any of it.

At the end of the party he watched as Thomas Selwyn Brittan helped my mother on with her jacket. My father was not a jealous man. He understood that men married women other than my mother, and this puzzled him. So when Thomas Selwyn Brittan draped my mother's jacket around her bare shoulders, he experienced a stab in the chest that he assumed to be an attack of angina.

In the car driving home my father was miserable. He could not blot from his mind the sight of a broken jetliner landed safely in a cornfield after being piloted there by an impeccably dressed Thomas Selwyn Brittan. He looked forlornly at my mother, who yawned.

"That Tommy what's-his-name was interesting."

"*Tommy!*" he cried. He had no idea things had progressed this far.

"Did you know he once landed a crippled passenger plane in a —"

"Yes yes, a cornfield. I know all that."

"No, a *minefield*! He landed a crippled plane in a minefield.

Imagine that. It was in Indochina eight years ago. They say the cockpit was on fire and he was being shot at!"

"I thought it was a cornfield."

"Oh, he did that too," she said cheerfully.

My father considered driving the car into a large oak tree, but at the last moment swerved away.

"Careful dear, you nearly hit that tree. Anyway, he had some very salient things to say about the aviation industry."

THAT NIGHT WHEN he took his position in bed my father felt a gulf between them. He woke up the next morning with a rash on his neck. By the end of the week his hair was falling out. At work he cut himself on a jigsaw and required eleven stitches. My mother took these changes in stride. From her reading at the library and from her discussions with Stella Davenport in particular, she knew that men were likely to fall apart at any moment. "Just a matter of time," explained Stella.

After two weeks of hair loss, my father grew determined to do something. At night, with my mother asleep, he crept out of their bed into what they both called her "study": a small, unused bedroom containing a Singer sewing machine, a typewriter, stacks of magazines with smiling women on the covers, and a book from the library by Jean-Paul Sartre titled *The Transcendence of the Ego*. Next to it sat the second deluxe unabridged Universal Webster's.

Until that point my father had considered all books to be instructional manuals of one kind or another, and was perplexed when he failed to find a section titled "Salient: Problems Caused By." Instead he found a crushing number of words that began with the letter S. *Salad, salad days, salad dressing, salading,*

salagane (same as salangane). The difference between "salaman-
drine" and "salamandroid" eluded him. In my father's mind
you either resembled a salamander or you didn't. He saw that
"Salian" was in fact a "Salian Frank," but this didn't help.

After cleaving his way through *Salicylide*, *salicylism* and *sali-*
cylous he hit the motherlode: "salience (or sal-yuns) n.1." His
heart thumped. "Salience: the state or quality of being salient."
Yes, that was it. *Saliency*, *salient*. That salient meant a heraldic
lion or other beast in a jumping posture with its forepaws on the
dexter point and back legs on the sinister part of the escutcheons, my father had no idea. He imagined Thomas Selwyn
Brittan in full armour with his fingers on the dexter point, and
a pair of two-hundred-dollar Italian leather dancing shoes,
resting on the escutcheons. He read on. "Salient: to spring
forth, leap." Yes, that was it. That was something that appealed
to women: to spring forth, to "leap about like a stag." Now he
was getting somewhere. "2. Salient: the part of a battleline
or fort, etc. that projects furthest toward the enemy. 3. To be
noticeable, conspicuous, to stand out from the rest, to jut out at
an angle, to caper, to gush, to be in a state of jetting forth." My
father moaned and shut the dictionary.

FOR THE FIRST time in his life he fell asleep on the sofa in front of
the television. Dirt appeared under his fingernails. He snored
without repentance. At dinner my mother, after considering her
words carefully, asked if something was the matter.

"No, nothing's the matter. It's just ... why don't you make
lamb shanks anymore?" he shouted.

"Dear, you're eating lamb shanks."

"Well," he said, "they're delicious."

"Thank you," she said. He'd fallen apart just like Stella said he would.

My father remained in that condition for a week. Several times he drove his forehead into the crook of his elbow and moaned. He began to sweat when my mother left the room, suspecting her of taking dance lessons at the Thomas Selwyn Brittan dance studio. Ten times a day he reminded himself that he was not salient.

"I'm not salient," he muttered.

"What's that, darling?" My mother entered the room with a plate of biscuits and plunked it on the side table. She had diagnosed my father's condition as a type of brain injury, and was treating it with a regimen of baked goods.

They sat and watched a show on television. Every few moments the laugh track roared, indicating something funny had taken place. My father couldn't stand it anymore.

"Jean."

My mother was not accustomed to hearing him speak her name, and looked at him strangely. He called her "darling, dear, sweetie, sweet pea, and sugar jar." He called her "honey, bunny, and sunny," and sometimes he called her "my little cabbage" in the belief that he was using a translation of a common French endearment. Under almost no circumstances did he call her Jean.

"Jean, I'm going out." With that he put his coat on and swept out the door.

MY FATHER SWEPT exactly four blocks to the nearest tavern where he hoped to find Harold Currie, a known poet. Two years earlier the man had ordered a custom-made writing desk from my father and neglected to pay for it. He spotted Harold in the corner behind an immense stein of beer, wearing a green croupier's vest and being abused by a furious dark-haired woman who seemed to be smoking two cigarettes at the same time. As my father approached, the woman peeled away from the table, stormed off, and checked him into the wall.

"Excuse *you*," she jeered.

My father regained his feet and approached the table.

"Bill," shouted the poet. "Sit the hell down."

No sooner had he sat down than a mug of beer appeared at his elbow.

"Harold, my wife's in love with salient."

The poet nodded. Nothing surprised him anymore.

"I mean the word, the word salient. She's in love with it."

The poet nodded again, this time stroking his beard. "As an adjective?" he asked piercingly. "Or a noun?"

"Adjective, noun? For God's sake, Harold, I'm a carpenter."

"Okay, Bill. I've dealt with this sort of thing before. It's more common than you'd think." Two weeks earlier Harold had knocked off a *terza rima* for a woman smitten by the word "sobriquet." In the manner of Pythias he had composed a dactylic hexameter for a fifty-year-old pest exterminator in which the word "stridulation" appeared five times, once for each decade of the man's life. There was nothing he would not do in the service of language.

"I'd pay you," pleaded my father, tugging at his wallet and producing two tens.

"That won't be necessary," said the poet, snapping the bills into a vest pocket.

Behind the poet's back my father saw a blond-haired woman

staring at them with smouldering fury. She seemed on the verge of crossing the floor and smashing Harold Currie in the face with a beer stein.

"Who's that woman? Does she know you?"

"Sheila," said the poet without turning around. Sheila Dunston. What a flower she is. A real *fleur du mal*."

"She looks like she wants to kill you."

"That's a woman's passion there, Bill. Unadulterated womanly passion."

"Harold, can you do anything?" My father was nearly in tears.

The poet squinted. "A sonnet might do it."

My father had a soft spot for professional terminology and warmed to what he was hearing. "Sonnet? When?"

"Tomorrow, come back tomorrow."

"Tomorrow? Don't you have to leap around first like a stag, or something? Or build a fort?"

The poet gravely tapped his temple. "I've got everything I need right here."

My father stood up, shook Harold Currie's hand, and swept out of the tavern the way he had swept into it.

THE NEXT EVENING he re-swept himself back to the tavern and found Harold Currie sitting at the same glossy black table with a mug of beer at his elbow. The poet delved into one of the many pockets in his vest, removed a business envelope, slapped it down, and pinged it across the table with his forefinger.

"Is it … a sonnet?"

Harold frowned. "I tried the sonnet, Bill, I did. Sonnets are good, but they're not good for everything. I mean, they're not a blank cheque, are they?"

"No I ... I guess they're not."

"What we really need to do is cut to the chase. For that you need a quatrain."

"A quatrain?" My father could barely conceal his disappointment.

"Quatrain. Absolutely. The last thing we want to do here, Bill, is lose focus. That's the weakness of the sonnet. It's prone to drifting. For you, the quatrain is the way to go."

"You think so?"

"I don't think so, Bill, I know it."

My father nodded. He was starting to gain confidence in the quatrain already.

"How long will it take?"

"That's the beauty of the quatrain. You'll see improvements right away. Deep-rooted core stuff might take longer — two, three days, I'm not sure. By the end of the week your wife'll be good as new. Take it home, Bill, spruce it up, put a ribbon around the envelope. She'll be begging you for mercy."

My father did not appear convinced.

"Trust me," said Harold, "I'm a poet."

MY FATHER DID more than put a ribbon around the envelope. He constructed an eight-and-a-half-inch frame from black walnut, cut a glass sheet cover, and had the secretary at work re-type the quatrain on her IBM Selectric. She thoughtfully double-struck each letter for him.

The following day, after a serving of lamb shanks, my father presented his package to my mother.

"For me?" she said innocently, tugging at the coloured paper, relieved to find that he had not given her another framed photograph of herself.

"It's a quatrain!" shouted my father.

My mother's lips parted. "Bill," she said, and read it out loud.

IN PRAISE OF A SALIENT WOMAN
Forget the schmucks who came and went
Who read some books but were not intent
On YOU, my wife, furnace of my contentment
Who stokes my life and makes it salient.

"Oh, Bill, *that's* definitely going up on the wall." She got up and immediately fastened the frame above their bed with an upholstery tack.

That night my parents turned off the television before the weather was completely over. In bed, my father felt his arms to be as strong as oak trees. His lips extended like the perimeter of a fort. His chest leapt like a stag. He was in a state of jetting forth, of capering in all directions. My father was noticeable. He stood out. He was conspicuous.

Nine months later they had me.

Back Then

DOWN THE STREET from me lived a witch or a crazy woman. When we were children we went to her house and found ways to be cruel to her. From beneath a hedge, or behind the trunk of the chestnut tree in my front yard, I watched Steve Bodegan and Al and Maxie Dunnigan tromped up her porch and hammer away at her door until something happened.

What happened was that she came to the door and began to scream at them, although in fairness there were other times when she opened the door and handed out cookies from a plate. Probably she wasn't crazy at all, probably she was entirely normal; just a lonely, beleaguered woman whose name I can't remember, and who got called "Old Lady" something-or-other simply because back then if you were female and over sixteen years old, we called you "Old Lady" something-or-other. Whatever she was, she lived in a house by herself and back then, if a woman did that, it was all anyone needed to know about her.

My own theory about this woman was that she had tripped over something in her life and never got back up. Maxie's mom was like that; a lot of people were like that. Maxie lived next door to me, and one morning I saw his mother brought home in a police car. I watched the whole thing from behind the chestnut tree, where I watched just about everything. They brought her home, helped her from the back seat of the cruiser, and when she got out I saw blood streaming from her nose, and she was laughing in a more witch-like way than Old Lady what's-her-name ever laughed. I'd never known a woman to make a sound like that before, and I'd never seen one step out of a cruiser with a bloody nose either, not even on TV.

Then there was the birthday party when Maxie's mom was sitting on a sofa in the Dunnigan's house, or maybe the Bates's place, and she peed herself. She stood up from the sofa and a dark circular stain showed on the cushion beneath her. The room went silent. Our parents stood there somewhere between their drinks and cigarettes, and the music of Perry Como coming from the hi-fi, and then went in a confused way into the kitchen where they started to whisper. Someone helped Maxie's mom to the door. We were kids back then and we had to fathom this thing on our own. It was a new place to us, where mothers peed themselves on the sofa and stumbled out of police cars with bloody noses. It seemed there was a lot of tripping and falling going on.

WHEN WE WEREN'T trying to figure things like this out, or pestering the crazy woman down the street, we roamed the neighbourhoods in search of chestnuts to knock down and make kingers with. If you were lucky your mother heated them in the oven for you to make them harder. We were also in search of baseball. The game of baseball kept watch over us like the best uncle you could have. We submitted to its rules without complaining. We threw, we caught, and we ran, until a sulking man named Mr. Cooper burst out of his house, stole our ball off his front lawn, and ordered us, or tried to order us, off the street. From the street we fanned out onto empty industrial lots, carrying baseball bats over our shoulders. Sometimes we chalked strike zones against the brick walls of schools and hurled tennis balls into them.

I played baseball with Gordy Davenport, Peter Moffat, and the Dunnigan brothers, and sometimes I played with Wally Maracle, who was an Indian and lived four houses down. Wally wasn't an Indian like the kind we saw on television back then. There were lots of Indians on television back then, wearing feathers, shooting bows and arrows, whooping and torturing people for the simple pleasure of doing it. Wally didn't do anything like that, but he was still an Indian, even if he wasn't an Apache. From TV back then you understood that most Indians in the world were Apache. There was no hair-splitting to find the right name; Native, First Nations, Amerindians — there were just *Indians*, plain and simple, and more often than not they were Apaches.

I didn't know it at the time, but with the name of Maracle, little Wally from down the street had risen up from the lands of the Iroquois Confederacy, and was linked by blood to the defeat of the American army at Stoney Creek and Lundy's Lane. It was because of Wally's relatives, painted up for war, that we didn't have to sing "Yankee Doodle Dandy."

He lived like the rest of us beneath the shade of a chestnut tree in what we called a wartime bungalow, wrapped up in red insulbrick. His skin was the colour of caramel, he had short arms and thick black hair, and he stuttered and weighed more than boys our age were supposed to. The other odd thing about Wally was that his mother had gone away.

It turned out that Wally's mother had walked off into the blue sky of an Indian Summer, and was never seen again. She had recently given birth to her fourth child and after that she went away and Wally no longer had a mother. Wally was the only person I knew who didn't have a mother. A few times I heard people say "she's run off with another man." Women said this, friends of my mother. It was a phrase that intrigued me, spoken across fences by women holding laundry pegs in one hand, and a cigarette in the other. Sometimes it was uttered over frosted glasses of beer on Saturday, when the work was done and cribbage boards were brought out and clapped against plastic tables. I understood it in the literal sense. I saw a stranger — the dreaded stranger we were forever getting warned about; the one who snatches up children and molests them — standing in the shadow of a tree waiting for Wally's mother to come out of her house. The screen door opens, she skips down the front walkway and the two of them, holding hands, run off together across the street into the woods and never come back out. It looked promising to me, but somehow I understood it was a bad thing, an indecent thing. I understood this by the way the words were spoken; "She's run off with another man." A hint of womanly longing clung to this statement, followed by a silence that suggested to me that the women who said this weren't sure if it was bad because Wally's mother had run off with another man, or because *they* hadn't.

I never asked Wally why he didn't have a mother anymore, and he didn't bring it up. He got fatter and kids teased him about that. They teased him a lot; they teased him because he stuttered and maybe they teased him because he was an Indian although

I don't ever remember that. He got fatter, he got teased, and he got mad. He got mad a lot, and one day he picked up a garden hoe from his father's tool shed and threw it at me.

I saw everything. I saw Wally step from behind the tool shed with a hoe in his hand. He held it, balanced it, and then for reasons that were not clear to me, or even to him, he reached back and heaved the thing. The hoe followed a slow arc through the afternoon sky, seemed to hang there for a moment, as though it could not make up its mind what to do, and finally fell at a leisurely pace and stuck itself into my leg just above the ankle. A bloody wound, shaped like a cross, flowered instantly. I still have the scar.

At the age of eleven, I followed Wally Maracle into a neighbour's backyard and climbed through the basement window of the Sullivans' house. The Sullivans were a tough brood of east coast kids with red hair who played tackle football, broke windows, and put tacks under your bicycle tires. They were gone for the summer, all of them, the whole family. Each summer they went back east.

I stood beside Wally in their basement and felt a strange, creepy sensation, as though the house was looking me over very carefully. Something had changed, something close to me. It took me a moment to realize what it was: I had become a criminal. Without even trying I'd crossed over the threshold into a life of crime. I'd followed Wally down the path of his childish vandalism into the dark of someone else's house and now a life of violent crime waited for me in a basement behind a shut door next to the furnace.

Without waiting for Wally, I got out of there as fast as I could, scrambling through the window into the sunlight and the shade of the chestnut trees, where it was safe. Wally stayed behind. He stayed in the basement foraging in the dark corners of the place, looking for all the fabulous things that must exist in a house that is not your house; the skateboards and the jars of peanut butter, the baseball gloves wrapped in twine to mould the pocket. He was twelve years old and he stood alone in that empty basement, searching for the things that were lost to him.

A FEW YEARS later Wally attempted to murder me with a cue ball at the local pool room. We were engaged in the late stages of a life-and-death snooker game, both of us smoking mentholated cigarettes in the casual manner of boys who know they are now grown up. The game had come down to the black ball. The loser paid the table fees. I shot ferociously, with all my might, sending the ball bouncing randomly around the green slate of the snooker table. It settled in a corner pocket — which meant I won. It also meant Wally Maracle had to pay. The rules were simple: the loser paid, Wally was the loser. A spasm of rage flew across his face. If there was one thing he understood, it was that the loser paid. His face trembled with the hatred of everything, even of me, especially me. He snatched the cue ball off the table and flung it at me. I ducked — swiftly, neatly — and the ball bulleted beside my ear, cracking the wall panel behind me. The owner of the place came out from behind a booth and yelled at us.

Some time after that I met Wally coming out from the parking lot of the baseball field where a dead tractor had lain for many years, a rusting heap of yellow steel now. We greeted each other guardedly. I was a fully grown sixteen-year-old, and he was a little older and fully obese. Wally stopped and held up his fingers for me to inspect. I saw the tips of them covered with sticky black ink, the thumbs in particular.

"They fingerprinted me," he said proudly. "I did a B and E." The code-words of his delinquency slipped importantly from Wally's mouth. I nodded at him but had only a vague idea what he meant. The police had taken him to the station and finger-printed him for some theft or another, and now his fingertips were covered in black ink. He kept his hands in front of him as if he intended never to let them down.

TEN YEARS LATER I came back to town because Pete Moffat was get-ting married and for some reason wanted me there to witness it. The wedding party marched in behind a Scottish bagpiper. The bride had a vivid smile and a broken tooth, and the drinking started early. By ten o'clock Pete had turned mean; his tie was off and he was reeling from man to man, looking for a fight. The bride was as drunk as Pete and had actually managed to get in a fight; she slapped a dark-haired woman in the face, called her a slut, and threw a wild right that missed. Later I watched her father grind out a cigarette butt on the lobby carpet in front of the staff. He seemed to think it was funny to do that, and it was clear to me that he was spoiling for a fight too.

Around midnight I stepped out the back of the hall with the Dunnigan brothers and we passed a joint around. Roy was now a boilermaker and married to a girl he made unkind jokes about, and Vic, the other one, was headed to a minimum security prison in Joyceville for a four-month stay, "vacation" he called it, and didn't seem too worried about the matter. It seemed he had done this sort of thing before. To make conversation I asked about Wally Maracle.

"Wally?" Roy examined the glowing end of a joint. "He's dead. You didn't know about that? A long time ago. It was in the papers."

"Yeah," said Vic, "it was in the papers. He climbed up a service road bridge over the highway near Oakville and jumped off into the traffic. He killed himself. Got run over by a truck."

"He got run over by more than a truck," said Roy. "Holy shit. He wasn't dead at first, right? Got run over by all sorts of things. What a mess. It was in the papers."

"Yeah, killed himself," said Roy, coughing up a chestful of smoke. "He was Indian, you know."

"Yes," I said, "I knew that."

WE TALKED ABOUT Wally Maracle for a while longer, and we talked about other kids we'd grown up with. It seemed they were all married now or divorced. Some were in prison, and some were dead: one had been shot in the spine during a card game and was paralyzed. A baby-faced kid named Christopher had killed his wife with a knife. Stanley Doyle had been deported to England. Someone else had been crushed at the steel plant. Those of us who had paper routes and put chestnuts on shoe laces, and played baseball on the street — me and Gordy and Pete and Vic and Phil and Wally — we were all grown up now.

Getaway Man

BODEGAN TURNED THE engine off and sat in the car counting to ten. At ten he turned the engine on again, then switched it off, but kept the radio on this time. In a high, unembarrassed voice he sang, out of tune with the singer, "*these eyes ...*" He sang along with the singer about the eyes of a girl, the eyes of a boy, wise and special eyes that had seen everything there was to see, like Bodegan had.

In the rear-view mirror he checked to make sure that no one was coming yet and then inspected the crest of his hair that swept forward in a way that was fascinating to him, and to girls too. Bodegan grinned at himself. He was extremely good looking. All he had to do was snap the lick of hair above his forehead and he could make a girl take her jeans off or lift up her shirt for him. Not just to feel her up either. Bodegan would go all the way; it was no big deal to him.

With his hands clamped on the steering wheel he admired the soft blond hairs sprouting from his arms. He could have any girl he wanted, and not just Penny Blandin either, who was still a skinny kid, really.

Bodegan punched hard at the radio and got another song. This one was about a moon on the rise, a bad moon. Looking out the windshield he scanned the sky but saw no moon or stars, only TV antennas leaning like black crosses against the night, and black wires running into the trees and coming out the other side. Bodegan lit a cigarette and saw that he had one already burning in the ashtray.

"Shit," he said coolly in a measured voice, pretending for a moment that a girl was in the other seat, evaluating everything he did and said. He swivelled and put his right foot on the passenger seat, where there was no girl at all. From there he studied the houses set back on the street: dull solid houses with dull people inside them and trimmed hedges and fences and kids who did their homework and kept hamsters in cages. He grinned, then butted the cigarette along with the first one and checked to see if his hand was shaking.

Bodegan didn't know what to do with himself. He flipped the engine on again so that it was already running when they came out. The sound burst from the hood and roared back at him. He wondered if people were coming to their windows to see what the noise was about; an old lady peering through curtains and writing down the licence number; the phone in her hand, dialing the cops.

He punched up and down the radio but couldn't find anything decent except commercials and people talking on the phone-ins. "Stainmaster," said a voice. "Exactly what you need for your interior and exterior household needs." He snapped it off. What he needed was a song; the right song to play along with the things he had done on the track and the playing field. There had been a time when he was an athlete. People knew that about him. Two years ago, when he was in school, his track shoes crunched on the cinder, and he came up to the high jump bar at the meet in Cayuga and cleared more air than anyone had seen before. Five foot seven. A record. The moment replayed itself in his eyes: the high bar, the thick blue mattress that waited on the ground … The school cheerleaders in their skirts, their hair swinging from side to side. It gave him no satisfaction now. Without music it disappeared into the concrete stairs leading to the basement of the house across the street with the garden hose left out on the lawn. Al and Maxie were down there doing a job. He imagined them working on the old man quickly, like professionals. They had him flipping up the cushions on the sofa to show them where all his money was stashed. "Sure guys, you can have it. Have it all," like they were doing him a big favour by robbing him of his money.

Bodegan grinned. He wondered if they'd bother to tie the guy up or not. He was a small, skinny man, on disability for something that happened in the mills a long time ago; an accident that no one knew about anymore. Chucky, they called him. His name was Chucky. "I got disability," he bragged, his voice thick and slurry, the way people talked when they had some pieces missing. He didn't work at the mill anymore. He didn't do anything that anyone knew, except that once Bodegan had seen him dressed up for the Boy Scouts with a green shirt on and a red scarf tied around his neck, walking down the street in a pair of brown shorts, like he was proud of it. All he did now was wait for the young guys to get off shift from the steel mill. They'd knock on his door after midnight when the banks were closed, and he cashed their cheques for them. He'd do it when the banks were open too. All you had to do was sign the cheque on the back, and sit there listening to him yak about what it was like in the old days before the union got in. He'd give you beer if you wanted it. A lonely guy who wanted company. "Like taking money from a homo," Maxie had explained.

BODEGAN SNAPPED HIS fingers, and as he did that two black figures passed behind him, across the mirror. Al came to the passenger's side at the front and yanked it open. He had a baseball cap on and there was sweat on his face. Maxie tumbled into the back and thumped the butt end of the baseball bat on the floor.

"Get out of here."

"Turn the car on," shouted Al. He swivelled to Maxie, who was singing something strange in the back seat. "He doesn't have the car on."

Bodegan turned the keys and the engine caught right off.

"It made too much noise. It sounded weird, so I turned it off." His voice rang higher than he wanted.

"Yeah?" said Al.

"Yeah," said Bodegan.

"Did it make too much noise?"

"Yeah, it did."

"Did it sound weird?"

"It sounded weird having the car running like that for no reason." Bodegan put the car in gear. "What, you want some old lady calling the cops?"

"Is that right? You call the cops?"

"What are you talking about?" Bodegan had driven off the street now onto a bigger one with maple trees overhanging the sidewalks, and street lights burning into the black. He heard Maxie in the back, breathing hard, as if he'd just finished running a race. Without looking he knew that Al was still staring at him.

Bodegan realized suddenly that he didn't like Al, and that he'd never liked Al. He didn't like his skinny pink lips, and the way his teeth leaned into his mouth. He didn't like the way he punched himself on his own knees. He checked Maxie in the rear-view. Maxie was okay; Maxie had stolen cars. The baseball bat was upright between his knees with the handle on top. His head was bobbing as he tried to line up a cigarette to his lighter.

Bodegan wanted to get rid of the feeling that was with him inside the car now and made an effort to think of the things he could do with money. First he'd buy something for Penny Blandin. Get her a bicycle, maybe. He smiled. A bicycle with a bell on it, and streamers coming out from the handle grips. That was funny.

"You get the money?" he said.

"Sure," said Al.

"We got the money, didn't we, Maxie?"

"I killed him," Maxie said quietly.

Bodegan laughed. "You got the money?"

"There wasn't any money," said Al.

"What do you mean? The money was in the sofa. Right?"

"There was no sofa."

"There was no money," said Al. "There wasn't even a sofa. He didn't have a sofa." Suddenly Maxie thumped the car ceiling with the butt end of the bat. Then he screamed a high teenage jolt of adrenalin and shoved his face up between the front seats.

"I killed him, didn't I, Al?"

"You smashed him, man."

"Yeah. I smashed him."

Bodegan struggled to keep his face pointed at the road. He saw Al turn sideways, grinning at Maxie, and was aware there was something between them that he wanted for himself, and couldn't get; the closeness of soldiers who did things together that were dangerous. It was near to him, like the smell of upholstery in the car; a dry vinyl smell of used cars, and cigarettes, and engine oil, and something else too; the smell of piss, a whiff of it, unmistakable, like his sister's diaper when she was a baby.

"I smashed his head, Al." Maxie leaned forward between the seats, holding the baseball bat in front of him. "I did, man. I smashed it so hard."

Bodegan saw the bat head suspended off his right shoulder, an aluminum bat with writing on it and a thick stain that looked like gravy. There were black hairs on the bat, hairs, stuck to the blood, the way hairs stuck to his hand after he stroked a cat. Chucky's hairs, he thought. Chucky. It seemed intensely strange that those hairs were there.

"You should've seen it, man. His head was there. His head was there, wasn't it, Al? It was in front of me, like ..." Maxie tipped the bat forward in between them to show what it was like. "He kept saying, 'I don't got none guys, guys, I don't got no money. I got beer. You want a beer?' 'Fuck you,' I said, 'we don't want beer, do we, Al? We want the money.' And that's when he went weird. He started whimpering, man, like a homo."

"Maxie whacked him."

"Yeah. I whacked him on the head, man. Full."

In the mirror Bodegan saw Maxie's arms fly back over his head, like he was demonstrating how to chop wood with an axe.

"I smashed him, man. I smashed him, eh? Like … You shoulda seen his face. His face." Maxie went silent. Bodegan sought him out again in the mirror and saw that his eyes were wide open and his lips had stopped moving.

"His face folded up, didn't it, Al? Folded up, man." Maxie slumped back and began to cry. He was sobbing like a little boy. Al slapped his hands on his knees, louder than before.

"You smashed his face." He looked straight ahead. "You did a job, man. You hit a homer off Chucky's head." He began to giggle foolishly.

Bodegan smelled the urine now like a bleach bottle with the lid off. Maxie was crying. Al slapped his hands on his knees.

Bodegan squeezed the wheel. His fingers were bone white. The blood had collected below his knuckles in little sacs that didn't seem to belong to him.

In front of him the road raced beneath the hood, the single broken white line creased the middle of it. Wires crossed overhead in pairs. The garbage cans were out by the curbs, ready for the trucks that would come in the morning. Beyond them shone the lights of the houses, thick and soft behind the curtains. Every room looked as cozy as a Halloween pumpkin with a candle in it. Girls were in there brushing their hair. Bodegan heard the sound of static, and even saw the blue sparks leap from the hairbrush to the shining filaments.

The road kept coming. Next to him, Al slapped his hands on his knees, like a bongo player, his chest rising and falling with each beat. Bodegan wondered why the radio wasn't playing anymore. There had been a song on the radio about a girl's eyes. He remembered the eyes of girls, and he remembered his track shoes on the cinder and his legs loose, as he circled for the jump.

A group of girls cheered his name. *Bodegan, Stevie Bodegan*. The music played and for a moment he saw the blue foam mattress on the ground in front of him, waiting to break his fall.

Halloween

IF YOUNG MRS. RIORDAN wore a wool toque with a fuzzy red tassel hanging down on either side of her face and the Charlie Chaplin moustache glued to her upper lip had begun to peel away, and a white Cinderella gown showed beneath her coat, and a pair of black fishnet stockings showed beneath that, then in all likelihood it was Halloween and there would be a spat of some sort.

The likelihood of a spat increased if Toby Riordan stood on the sidewalk a few steps behind his wife, fingering the stem of a wine glass that had once been full and now was pointedly not full. If he was directing his Celtic baritone into the glow of a cellphone and arranging to meet a co-worker at the Reckless Rhino Gentleman's Club to watch a girl named Brandy Ever-After wrestle a similarly named girl in a giant bowl of Jell-O, the chance of a spat increased considerably; and if, like Martin Skidmore, you were hopelessly in love with Mrs. Riordan, and standing in the doorway of your front porch after handing out a noticeably generous portion of chocolates and anonymous sugary things to both the Riordan daughters who were angels, probably you would yell out enthusiastically to Mrs. Riordan, "Your girls look fabulous." And because, like Martin, you had nothing to lose, you would add, "And *you* look fabulous too."

And because Mrs. Riordan was who she was, she would make a pretty and indeterminate expression with her lovely face and break into an enormous smile and say, "Oh thank you," as if this was the first time in her entire life that a man had thought to compliment her on her good looks. In fact, it was not the first time in her life that a man had thought to do that; it was not even the first time *recently* that a man had thought to do that. Fifteen minutes ago Ted Wheatly at 117 had said, "You look absolutely stunning." Mike Tomkinson at 119 had answered the door and said, simply, "Jesus Christ." At 121 Kristen Connelly's husband, who was literary, had opened the door, examined her from top to bottom and then back up again and said, "Let me guess, Helen of Troy?" Dana Swan had swaggered up to her on the sidewalk and, with the smell of special stock whisky on his breath, whispered, "Do you have a licence to wear those stockings?" to all of which Mrs. Riordan made a pretty and indeterminate expression with her face.

"I am so in love with you," thought Martin, forlornly, although he knew that he was not really in love with her at all but in love with her beauty, which was perhaps the same thing, or perhaps it wasn't. Despite this, he was forced to admit that even if Mrs. Riordan's husband was a premature drunk who would rather watch naked women squirm around in a vat of Jell-O instead of reading *The Berenstain Bears* to his children, he still had it all over Martin.

Recently, and with noticeable relief, Martin had come to admit to himself that he was a total failure. A washed-up writer of passionate historical articles that had once appeared in numerous magazines but were now appearing for free on the Internet, and without his permission. His books were remaindered before they made it out of the boxes. Only recently had his agent stopped muttering darkly about what she called "the death of the book," but instead was now making desperate and unconvincing pleas for what she had started to call "the resurrection of the book." His editor, a young woman with fine instincts for prosody in general, was in hospital in serious condition after getting struck down at a pedestrian crosswalk by a sixteen-year-old girl driving her father's car and texting her boyfriend at the same time.

Everything, absolutely everything, looked bad. At least it did not look good, beyond, of course, young Mrs. Riordan who looked fabulous. How much of life, thought Martin, was contained in the floating flecks of green that swam in Mrs. Riordan's irises? It was true that similar flecks of green swam in his wife's eyes; once they had been fantastic to him in the extreme, he had pursued his wife by land, sea, on foot, bicycle, and finally across the San Bernardino mountain range in a defective ultralight. He had in fact made that woman his wife. If not his "wife," for they had eschewed that sort of language, then the woman whom he had lived with for a considerable number of years and was now the mother of his children.

"Have a nice evening," Martin shouted idiotically into the back of Mrs. Riordan. What an idiot you are, he told himself, and watched Mrs. Riordan manoeuvre her two angelic children up the street past the flow of dads, all of whom were staring intently into their phones, but who managed to pull themselves away from their phones to stare intently at Mrs. Riordan, which they did from the ground up and then, without exception said, "Wow, you look great." To which Mrs. Riordan said thank you and did the pretty indeterminate-expression-thingy with her face.

In that moment it seemed to Martin he should take himself out of the house and put an end to his life. He pondered taking the subway to Broadview station and jumping off the Bloor Street viaduct into the traffic below like that other writer had done several years before. It was an oddly appealing plan, but it was not a realistic one. If Martin was to kill himself, who would coach his daughter's baseball team? Who would do the dishes and sort the recyclables? Who, he wondered, would take back his library books? And who, for that matter, would respond to his fan mail? Every year at Easter he received a letter from an elderly woman in a nursing home in East Anglia who wanted to know when his next novel was coming out, and each Easter Martin faithfully wrote to her and explained that she had mixed him up with the British writer named Martin Skidmore and that in fact he did not write novels. Martin smiled in spite of everything. He was not the sort of person who killed himself. Or wrote novels.

Martin stood silhouetted in the doorway of his house and handed out candies to small pirates, princesses, bumblebees, video drones, and a few surly, uncomfortable-looking teen-agers who, as far as Martin could tell, were not anything at all. The street surged with ten-year-old robots wrapped from head to foot in aluminum foil, and eager little boys dressed elabo-rately as the characters in video games that Martin had never heard of. Up the street a way, he made out the athletic back of Toby Riordan as he followed his wife up the block. Martin took some satisfaction in seeing that an eruption of plaster showed on his chin where he had cut himself shaving. Last Halloween it had been a large bruise beneath his right eye that, according to Toby, had appeared under hazy circumstances following drinks with a former goaltender for the Philadelphia Flyers.

"Trick or treat," piped a fuzzy, large-eared thing who was either a rabbit or a hamster or perhaps both. Martin unleashed a handful of hard candy into her plastic bucket and heard it land like spent bullets.

"Say thank you. Did you say thank you?" This plea came from a dark, grim-sounding figure on the sidewalk.

"Thank you," said the girl and shuffled off the porch with the slow, solemn dignity of a general in uniform.

HALLOWEEN FLOWED LIKE a great pagan festival beneath the street lights and the moon and the branches of the trees and Martin could not take his eyes off of it. There went Mrs. Riordan out of view, stopping traffic with her stockings and her smile. Toby, at her back, with the grin, was already anticipating drinks at a gaudy club where the girls wrestled in Jell-O. Across the street he saw Matthew, whose last name was unknown to him, a bearded, sessional professor of linguistics with a passion for Scottish dance and inexpensive rum, wearing the same flamboyant velvet green kilt he did each Halloween. His permanently indignant wife, with the tight bun of grey hair, hovered next to him furiously handing out candies. She was a living, walking catalogue of man's stupidities and keen to share them with Martin or anyone who would listen. On the sidewalk Marcie Rennet, recently and dramatically divorced, steered her disconsolate fifteen-year-old daughter about the street in an attempt to bridge whatever difference had opened between them. Martin knew that the girl had been hospitalized recently for something ominous but he did not know what it was, although he suspected that the women in the neighbourhood did and they weren't telling, at least not the men. Marcie laughed and called out cheerfully to the people she recognized. The daughter was sullen and filled with rage and dressed in the costume of the latest transgressive female superstar singer who Martin had never heard of.

They came fast and thick; angelic girls dressed as angels, held aloft by their mother's makeup and wings made out of coat hangers; devilish boys dressed as devils, armed with plastic satanic pitchforks; a swarm of zombies and vampires, no end of zombies and vampires this year, tottering on the sidewalk, flashing plastic teeth, dripping blood and laughing. Martin, in a moment of clarity, realized that each of them was searching for sweetness. That's what it was. Every zombie, every vampire, every transgressive female hip-hop superstar look-alike was marching up and down, door to door, in search of sweetness. It was always that.

He saw Larry Hershfield, the translator whose daughter was in remission now but who during the worst of it had stood next to Martin on the schoolyard and stared into the trees and pointed out how the sunlight struck the leaves and how he would cling forever to the sunlight that struck the leaves and came through the branches, and that nothing, nothing would ever defeat the sunlight that streamed through the leaves of the maple trees. Martin could not bear to look at Larry because he knew that the beautiful bald little girl would be dead by the end of the week, but in fact the girl did not die, she was alive, her hair was yellow and she was charging down the sidewalk in front of her dad. Larry had his crazy hat on and was talking eagerly to anyone who would listen to him.

"Larry," he yelled, but Larry didn't hear him.

He saw the little daughter of Marianna Scolla and then Marianna herself, the Argentinian stunner who had buried two husbands and was now living with a man half her age. Decades ago at the ripe age of seventeen she had found herself sitting on Dizzy Gillespie's knee at an after-hours club in Rochester and Martin thought longingly that the path of beautiful women was always strewn with such memories. Joe Bukowski passed in front of his view, the graphic designer and serious pot smoker who had not very long ago flown in a pound of hash oil from Amsterdam third class on an Air Canada flight while travelling with his wife, his kids, and his mother-in-law. Joe's own mother, Martin knew this, had drunk herself to death and was found by Joe in her apartment, dead in a grotesque position on the floor with a bottle of gin in her hand. Joe was waving his kids up onto the porches and hugging everyone in sight, especially Mrs. Riordan. He saw Angelina Kross, who had attempted suicide and was now the director of the Parkside Seniors' Home entertainment committee and who was so adored by her grandkids that they refused to venture up a single porch unless she came with them. She was eighty-one years old and it seemed to Martin that both she and Mrs. Riordan shopped for their stockings at the same store.

Don Charbonneau threw his fist into the air. "Comrade Skidmore," he shouted and grinned. Don had been tasered by the Mounties, tear-gassed in Montreal, handcuffed in Seattle, pepper-sprayed in Toronto, and had released a live dove into the council chambers of City Hall, for which he was fined twelve hundred dollars. His twin boys were dressed in the same little Ho Chi Minh outfits they were dressed in last year with red stars their mother had sewn on their caps. He heard the strident, unmistakable peal of Marilyn Preston's laugher, then saw her with her gang of children in tow. Marilyn's grandmother had survived a polar bear attack in a small boat in a lake in northern Labrador in 1959. Martin had written an article about it.

All of them, thought Martin, every one of them had survived polar bear attacks; polar bears and croup and kidney disease and cross-addicted husbands; teenage daughters posting naked pictures of themselves on the Internet; an octogenarian parent living in a ground floor apartment in their house with a dizzying number of medications that required taking, and failed marriages. Failed businesses, dreams that had died, plays that had flopped, stocks that had tumbled, best friends whose lives had ended violently in car crashes, dogs gone rabid, grown children who refused to talk to them, Crohn's disease, former lovers from twenty years ago who phoned suddenly out of the blue, bitter custody arrangements, massage parlours, bad teeth, fathers who raped them, clinically depressed mothers who forgot to feed them, incompetent surgeries. So many bad things in fact that Martin wondered how there could possibly be enough sweetness on the planet to fix it all.

And while he was thinking, two small children detached themselves from the stream that had thinned considerably by this time, both of them dragging an enormous sack behind them.

"Hi, Dad," said Alicia, the youngest.

"We scored big time," said Sara, the older one. They went subdued into the house and up the stairs. Their eyes were dull with exhaustion but he knew that in a moment they would have their glittering loot spilled on the living room carpet, that Alicia would be stacking, sub-dividing, and counting hers like a banker, and that Sara would have hers piled in a great heap, like pirates' treasure, staring dreamily at it.

Coming down the street he saw the top of a woman's head, familiar to him, like something from a dream he'd had many times. Her dark hair crested up and back in a way he had always associated with beauty in a woman, even as a boy, and beneath the crest of this hair he recognized the woman.

"You missed everything," she said excitedly, running up on to the porch. "You really did. My God, Marlene Riordan and that asshole husband of hers had a fight like you wouldn't believe. I mean an all-out screaming foul-mouthed fight on the corner of Galley and Spenser with the kids in tears, and her screaming in his face and him looking at her with that stupid grin of his and saying yeah yeah yeah. Jesus Christ. Everyone staring at them. What a mess. Really, those poor kids. It's amazing they do as well as they do."

She shook her head and put her arms intensely around his shoulders. She cleared her throat. She kissed him on the side of the face and went up the stairs to help the kids bank their loot.

Martin scanned the street. It was emptying fast. As quickly as they came, they went away. He knew the drill. In two minutes the street would be entirely empty and later the teenage boys would come and kick his pumpkin to bits.

What It Was

HESSLER PUSHED THE button on the answering machine, cleared his throat, and tried again. *You've reached Michael Hessler. I'm not in right now, but if you wait for the tone, leave your name, number, and marital status, I'll get right back to you.* That was better. He liked that, especially the bit about the marital status.

He left the phone machine, strode to the thermostat, and turned it up. There was no way he could get the place warm enough these days: an endless chill had wormed its way into the house and refused to leave, like the kind that afflicts the bones of very old people. He adjusted the dial, flicked it once with his finger, and sat down. The chair was comfortable but not comfortable enough. It was a decent chair though, considering he'd picked it out of someone's garbage before the truck came. It disgusted Hessler what people put out for garbage. He sat in it and wondered what was eating at him.

Probably it was women. It was Elise of the long legs, the almond eyes and the violently alcoholic father. But Elise was three months ago already. Why not Carolyn? Carolyn of the flute. Carolyn was hardly any time ago at all. Or Julia of the stained speakeasy couch? Or Ronnie, that girl Steve brought over, the Vancouver one who drank the Manhattans and had the tiger tattoo on her backside. He didn't have to do a thing for her. He just sat there in the same chair he was in now with a drink in his hand and she was all over him. That girl was messed up. Or Alison. If it wasn't for Alison he would not have had the fight with Elise, and Elise would not have thrown his four-hundred-dollar leather jacket on the street to get flattened by the garbage truck.

Hessler got up from the chair and opened the curtains. They were not the sort of curtains he would ever buy; lace things, intricately patterned; the kind he presumed old ladies were familiar with and discussed in soft, knowledgeable voices. The curtains belonged to his mother and he endured them for her sake. The house belonged to his mother too. He lived in it by himself; his mother lived in a condominium on the fifteenth floor overlooking the lake. He cut the lawn, thawed the pipes when they froze, and even paid some rent, but not very much.

HESSLER STOOD BY the window and watched his sister roll up with the U-Haul attached to the car — an enormous green Pontiac riding low to the ground, and a muffler that rattled on the pavement. He was expecting her and she was right on time, as always. Hessler had the very strong sensation that if he hadn't opened the curtains at that precise moment, she wouldn't have showed.

He watched the car back in, U-Haul first. A trailer wheel cut across the lawn and left a rut. He'd hear about that, from his mother. Finally they got the U-Haul backed up into the driveway and cut the engine.

His sister got out first and then Larry who was her new man. It seemed to Hessler that his sister was always bringing someone around named Larry. Larry got out of the car. He was one of the largest men Hessler had ever seen. He was so heavy that when he stepped from the car, the vehicle lifted up off the ground as though exhaling. Hessler did not have a lot of sympathy for people who were overweight. With some people it was the glands and he was willing to concede there was nothing you could do if it was in the glands. When it was glandular it was different and he was capable of sympathy. But with this guy it was not glandular. Hessler didn't know how he knew that, he just did. Maybe it was the tattoos on his arm, or the long, greasy ponytail that hung down his back. With this guy it was just being fat, and when you were that fat, it meant you drank too much beer and ate too much crap and were filled up with anger. That's what it was. Anger. Hessler was sure of it.

The kids got out last; two of them. They belonged to Larry, and looked around the place as though they'd landed in a foreign country. They looked like typical kids wearing big pants, sneakers that weren't done up, and caps on backwards. They were cool. They were so cool they could hardly stand it. At least they weren't fat.

Hessler took a good look at his sister's new man. His mother had filled him in already on the details; how he'd been evicted from his place, and had to move into a basement apartment. Only Larry, it turns out, was a collector, a regular Mr. Fix-It. So would Hessler mind if they came around and stored some of his things in the garage. In *mother's* garage, is how Rhonda put it. To Hessler's knowledge his sister had never gone on a date with a man without putting a down payment on a house for him, moving him into a trailer park, or financing his way through a correspondence course in aircraft mechanics. "I'm just helping him get on his feet," is how she put it.

Hessler shut the curtains. To listen to his sister you would've thought all men had been cut off at the ankles.

He stopped as he got to the door — something was definitely bothering him. Maybe it was Rhonda. Maybe that's what it was. He remembered her other guy, Perry, or was it Harry? She set Harry or Perry up in a trailer park and then he punched her out. He beat her up so bad that he got three years in jail for it. It was some kind of record. No one around here had ever received a three-year sentence for punching out his girlfriend before. It made the news. Suddenly his sister was the Olympic gold medal winner at getting punched out by boyfriends. Two years later Harry or Perry was out of jail and she starts to date him again. She wants to bring him around for Christmas dinner. She would have too, only Hessler put his foot down. Absolutely not. No Perry or Harry. She had the nerve to start crying about it over dinner. He slammed his fork down; "It's a good thing that guy didn't kill you," he said. "Or you'd have *married* him." And that was it. At that point the bag was open and the cat was out of it. Rhonda started bawling. "I'm just trying to help him get back on his feet." Then his mother was in on it too: "I hope you're pleased with yourself, Michael. You are just like your father." After that, Rhonda started crying even louder. If Daddy was here he would slap your face. If Daddy were here, Hessler reminded her, he would do a lot more than that. Only Daddy was not here because the last anyone saw of Daddy he had a bottle of Navy rum in his hand

and was sitting on the floor of an empty house after everyone had moved out on him. He was still sitting there for all anyone knew. Michael, you stop that! His mother was off again, so Hessler kept his mouth shut. But Christmas, she told him later, had been ruined.

HESSLER STEPPED OUTSIDE and greeted his sister.

"Rhonda."

"Michael. Michael, this is Larry."

The man pivoted on the driveway and turned to face him. Hessler saw that his nose was large and intersected with veins. He put out his hand and Hessler took it.

"So you're the brother, hey?" Larry laughed, as though he'd made a clever joke.

"That's right. I'm the brother." Hessler was glad to get his hand out of the guy's mitt. It was like having it sunk in a wad of pastry. He looked over at the two kids, and then looked away at nothing.

"Okay." His sister sighed, relieved. She was bustling around now, taking charge of everything. It got under Hessler's skin when she acted like that.

"Okay," she repeated, beaming with things to do. "Michael, this is Luke. Say hello, Luke."

The youngster named Luke shuffled over. He looked to be twelve, maybe thirteen with earphone wires dangling from his ears and a tinny, percussive noise emanating from his head. He wasn't comfortable. Hessler didn't blame him; he wasn't comfortable either.

"Nice to meet you, Luke." He was being cool about it, but before he could stop himself, his arm was out to shake the kid's hand. He knew better than to do that. They shook and sure enough Luke turned away and stared off to the horizon as though an imaginary shopping mall had been built there.

Rhonda beamed.

Having shaken hands with Luke, Hessler had no choice but to do the same with his brother. Reluctantly the boy put his arm up in front of him like a broken branch he'd picked up off the lawn.

"Micky, this is Michael."

"He knows that." Hessler barely touched the kid's hand.

"Hi, Micky."

"Yeah, hi." Micky looked even more uncomfortable than his brother.

There was a lull. No one said anything. Hessler was aware of a blue jay from somewhere far off, screeching into the afternoon.

Finally he cut in. "Okay, what do we have to do?"

He wanted to get down to the business at hand. He wanted his sister out of there as fast as possible, and her fat boyfriend too. The kids though, they were all right, he wouldn't mind having them around. Maybe there was a basketball in the garage? They could bounce that around for a while. In fact, he remembered there was a basketball in the garage, only it was flat, and Hessler didn't have a pump for it. He had a pump, but not the fitting for the valve.

"Yes." Rhonda beamed again. She was motivated. She had something to do. She was always happiest when she was helping men get back on their feet. "Larry's got a little side business going, a retail thing. You know, the flea markets." She looked over very proudly at her man. Larry looked pretty satisfied with himself too. "We'll just store some of it, you know, put some inventory in the garage for a while."

Hessler didn't say a word. Inventory. Even with a frayed, plastic tarp over top, and held down by stretch cords, he saw that it wasn't inventory. It was junk; busted black and white televisions, an eight-track cassette player, the shell from a clothes dryer. He'd bet there was an old Coke machine in there too; rigged up to dispense dew worms into Styrofoam coffee cups. Inventory —

"I mean, you've got room, don't you?"

Hessler looked at his sister carefully. They'd gone over all of this before.

"Sure. There's room."

"Good," she seemed relieved. "Larry, why don't you and the kids unhitch the trailer. Is ... is the door ..." She looked over at the garage door as though there might be something pornographic going on behind it.

"No. It's locked. I'll go in and open it."

"Good, yes, good. Thank you."

Then Larry went into action. "Luke, Micky, get over here. Help me. Help me get this trailer off."

Hessler went into the house and shut the door. His back was up. Probably it was having Rhonda around again, or that creepy, overweight boyfriend of hers. He went to the window and opened his mother's lace curtains. Larry was out there making a big show of getting the trailer off the hitch, rolling up his sleeves up and heaving one leg over the bar. He snapped at Luke.

"Jesus Christ, get over here!" Luke came over meekly and stood beside his father. "Pull," he ordered. "Pull." The two of them gave it a yank but nothing happened. "Pull on it, for chrissakes." They gave it another shot and this time the hitch came off the ball. Larry let it drop hard on the tarmac. Micky, the one without the earphones, had been standing by watching; now he went over to the front of the U-Haul and leaned against it. Luke came over and stood next to his brother. Larry wiped his hands on a rag that he yanked out of his back pocket, meticulously getting every speck of grease off his fingers. While he was occupied with doing that, he stepped back over the bar and leaned on the U-Haul.

The rest seemed to take place in slow motion. Hessler saw the trailer begin to roll. Micky stepped away and said something. Larry straightened up and looked back, too late to do anything. The trailer slammed against the garage door. It hardly made a noise at all but the door buckled and a deep diagonal crease crawled up the aluminum. That was it. Hessler wouldn't get the door open over the rollers anymore. Maybe if he was lucky, he could hammer it flat again, but he doubted it.

"For chrissakes, look what you did!" shouted Larry.

Suddenly his sister wasn't beaming. "Larry, what happened?"

"It was Micky. He was leaning on the trailer for chrissakes, Micky!"

"I didn't do nothing." Hessler heard the indignation rise up in the boy's voice. "I didn't do nothin'."

"Nothing? You did nothing? Don't tell me you did nothing." Then Larry slapped the kid hard, once, on the face.

HESSLER WASN'T IN the house anymore, he was outside on the driveway. He saw the boy Micky staring furiously at the tarmac. A red palm print, like a maple leaf, burned on his face. His brother looked up to the sky as though he wasn't there, and whistled the same note over and over.

"That was *your* fault." Hessler heard his own voice but it seemed to be coming from somewhere else. Somewhere where the blue jay was. "You did it. You leaned on the trailer. It was you. You did it."

"Michael."

"You did it. You leaned on the trailer, you broke the garage door and then you slapped your own kid. You slapped his face."

"Michael!"

"You don't ever come around my place and slap your kid's face."

"Yeah?" The man grinned at him. "Your place? See, I heard it wasn't your place. I heard you live here for free. I heard a lot about you. I heard —"

Hessler hit the man in the mouth very hard, a rubbery smack that felt like nothing and left a low percussive noise in the air, which meant some damage had been done. A bird squawked. A blue jay maybe. His sister screamed at him.

"Stop it, Michael, stop it!"

But Hessler knew he was a long way from doing that.

Black Book

HIS ADDRESS BOOK contained one complete address: Martin Sedges on a sycamore-lined street in East Stroudsburg, Pennsylvania, where he lived with a diabetic cat he injected twice daily, four children, and a wife who baked. Except for that single address it was a book of telephone numbers; scribbled, crammed together and crossed out. He'd had the thing for years, even before his marriage, but now the pages were beginning to fall away, like hair — his own hair, and like his marriage.

Recently the B's had gone missing, taking Bobovitch, Fred with them. Hessler, in a fury, had turned the house upside down looking for that page. Finally he gave up and called the operator for Fred's number. He'd known Fred for twenty-two years but had never committed the number to memory. Probably that meant something about their friendship, but Hessler was not sure what. Fred lived in the 766 exchange in the west end with a cat, a dog, two children, and a wife who did not bake. She ordered in. Tall, stately, and schizo affective, sometimes she threw her medication down the toilet and smashed things. Recently Fred had sat in Hessler's living room, blank and

disoriented, drinking *Sortilège* from a thin bottle and not saying anything. The kids were at Fred's father's again. Later,
Hessler and Fred walked out along the street, combing through
the used bookstores, turning flagrantly on the sidewalk to
admire the young women.

Hessler copied Fred's number down into his new book. He
saw already that this one would have fewer names in it. Maybe
that meant he had fewer friends, or maybe he had better ones.
Some of them were dead in accidents. One had stepped off his
apartment balcony in the middle of a Thanksgiving dinner.
Steven Craigleigh had disappeared into the interior of British
Columbia. He missed Craigleigh the most. A large, vibrant,
Gaelic homosexual with implausible hair, they met working in
the same office, and ate lunch together. At one point Hessler
stood up, strolled the length of the cafeteria and took a good
look at the girl from personnel, a redhead who sat alone with
her legs crossed, wearing flesh-coloured stockings. When he
returned Craigleigh said, "Excuse me, but that was the most
obvious cruise I've ever seen."

Hessler thought about it for a moment. "Yeah, well, that's
easy for you to say, isn't it?" They became fast friends but
Craigleigh was haunted by ghosts. At night he stalked rough
trade behind the oak trees in High Park. "You'll get killed,
like that other guy," Hessler warned him. "Nonsense. I've got
a whistle." Craigleigh flourished a stainless steel whistle on
a shoelace, as though it was a piece of armour that rendered
him invincible. Hessler envied his friend's many lovers. Sometimes Craigleigh went to a club called Home Boys and brought
two, three different men a night back to his apartment. He had
been disowned by his parents. In a crime that made the news,

his twin brother had handcuffed a man to a tree beside a train siding outside Marathon, Ontario and murdered him with a crossbow. Craigleigh's parents had not disowned *him*. Once a week Craigleigh received a letter from his brother, written from a maximum security cell in Kingston, Ontario, urging him to accept Christ the Saviour into his heart. Now Craigleigh had changed his name and was somewhere east of Quesnel, British Columbia, a dot on the map, hidden among the giant Sitkas, and he wasn't coming out. Hessler knew he would never see him again.

HESSLER SAT QUIETLY, like a student, transferring names and numbers from his old black book and writing them down into a new one. It was a gloomy experience and for some reason it reminded him of a day years ago, waiting to be seated at a restaurant, standing in front of an aquarium where a doomed lobster clattered against the glass, staring at him, begging, it seemed, for his help.

He'd given up on doing the thing alphabetically and allowed himself to drift among the C's. Canpress Photo ... Computer Sales and Rental ... Susan Casabian. Casabian? Hessler couldn't remember her at all. Julia Cunningham he could. Broad-bottomed, touchable, wrapped in a towel. She drank stout glasses of vermouth and preferred men from the Caribbean. In the past she had not always been treated with respect and had serious and, in Hessler's opinion, legitimate worries about a man who was about to be released from prison. Hessler had passed up an opportunity to sleep with her. Three months married, he found himself troubled by a traditional concept of fidelity. He had wondered where those qualms came from. Not his father. For the second time in five years Hessler's father was being sued for divorce by a flight attendant.

Sometimes at night he thought of Cunningham, Julia. The towel cinched between small breasts, two imprints of water pulsing on the tiles by her naked feet. A gram of hashish on the table. Her underwear draped on the back of a chair. Athletic thighs. She was a runner. Her legs beckoned to him like the runway of an airport.

"I passed up a chance to sleep with that woman because of you." Hessler, ungraciously, had found reason to say this to his wife. She was marking term papers. "What a hero you are," she said, without looking up.

Hessler copied the Cunningham number down.

Inexplicably among the D's, he found Evelyn Armstrong. They played baseball together. He thought he might be in love with her. She had lately married a tall, moody Mohawk who insisted he was directly related to the individuals who cut out Father Brebeuf's heart and ate it. Hessler copied the number.

McGrath, Terry. It was time to call Terry. Seven years ago he'd been struck by lightning while opening a door. His shoes smouldered on the carpet, and a filling fell out of a tooth. Otherwise he was fine. His son had a serious developmental handicap that was not expected to get any better. Hessler thought that he should call him.

Irene Motan. Her skin was the colour of creosote. Born in Dutch Guyana, she whispered to him about a childhood in which enormous snakes slithered through the yard, dragging away the family dog. Hessler had intended to visit her in the suburbs when he was especially needy. But the suburbs were a long way away. It hadn't worked.

THE C'S SADDENED him and so did the D's. For some reason he skipped to the Y's and W's, which only made things worse. Across those pages Jennifer Wheatly had strewn her excitable life, her many telephone numbers scattered up and down the final pages of his book, like tattoos on the arms of a basketball player. He remembered her place in Montreal; the black cast-iron staircases winding like pretzels out of the snow, bagels and baklava for breakfast, two high points of crimson on her cheeks. Montreal, Madrid, Ottawa ... All the 613 numbers, and that house she lived in on McLeod, with Gloria and Kirsten. Their names flew by like railway sidings. Youth, extreme youth and the stunning women with luminous eyes. Young women who went to Europe together, swam naked in a Roman cistern. They danced with Basque terrorists, allowed themselves to be kissed in archways envisioned by Gaudi. Eighty-year-old Spaniards without teeth crawled timelessly toward their sleeping bags. On the Villa Borghese they were offered diamonds by strangers. They wore their beauty as easily as an old sweater. In that house in Ottawa with the cupolas and the many cats, the couriers arrived, it seemed every day, bearing orchids from professors of literature and ambassadors from Latin American countries; married men with children who were willing to throw it all away to sit on the bed, to look in their eyes and watch them reach behind their backs and unfasten their brassieres. Hessler had watched Gloria toss the orchids into the fridge along with the rest of them, and in that gesture and in that orchid-filled fridge he saw the casual power of their beauty. Then it was gone. Jen was killed in a car crash; a stray letter came to him a day before the funeral. "I have been nothing but silly lately." Kirsten married an Eritrean who refused to allow her to answer the telephone. He didn't know what happened to Gloria. He had seen her on television recently, protesting something.

They had strewn themselves like jewels across two continents and now they were vanished, like girls on the street in summer. For a time their names and lives had meant something to him. Now there was nothing to transcribe of Jennifer anymore; that last number could be crossed out. It no longer applied. So many things didn't apply anymore; so many names had been crossed out; these women who aimed their perfect bodies at the sun and now nursed a codeine dependency and watched television in the afternoon.

Hessler fingered backwards to the G's. Esther Grafton. He copied three of her numbers: her home, her cell, and her office number. She lived with her new boyfriend now, a film editor, but did not sleep with him. For some reason Hessler clung to that detail. She didn't eat meat either; she ate miso and practised Ashtanga yoga. At his old place, on her knees, naked except for her bra hooked upside down around her waist, she grabbed him down to her, her face gleaming, and wild. "My husband just bought a rifle," she whispered.

Hessler was aware that something had pulled ahead of him; the gleaming flash of the stock car that finally overtook you in a race to the finish line. He had closed his eyes for one moment and now everything was different. Mike Tomkin lay on his back on the floor of a discotheque in Hull, reciting naughty lines from Chaucer. Now he lived in a large house where he stripped furniture, collected antique lead soldiers and wrote letters to the editor. He was happily married. Hessler had not spoken to him in four years.

FROM OUTSIDE CAME the sound of a shovel scraping on the sidewalk. The snow fell more thickly by the minute; the sort of snow that gummed up your eyelashes and swirled around the city, slowing it to a crawl. Far away he heard the faint whooping of a car alarm, like a bird, rising from a marsh. Sawchuk, Mark ... Stanford, Peter ... Leon, Karen. All he remembered was a voice. A breathless, obliging voice on a telephone. "You want to know what I've got on?" A symphony of voices on telephones. "Sometimes it's like you have no feelings." His wife said this to him on an evening that had gone wrong. "No feelings. Only hunger." She was crying, both of them intractable, each pressing to the wall of their own stubbornness. "You don't care about anyone, do you?" That old place they had arrived at once again. Hessler would not give an inch.

His wife had been a dancer once. An artist's model. There was nothing she hadn't been. Her old numbers still littered his book, a co-op in the market, shacked up with a rock band and a blind cat. A twenty-third floor balcony on Eglinton where one night an eagle flew in front of his face and looked him straight in the eye. As a young girl she had done the Mash Potato, the Elephant, perhaps even the Watusi, spun the bottle in carpeted rec rooms, played Twister in a two-piece bathing suit, and pressed against boys with very long hair. At university she slept with her professors, ran car keys along the length of a Corvette belonging to a jazz musician who had disappointed her. She brought drugs home to a man who sat cross-legged on a pillow and contemplated the Buddha. Years ago on Yonge Street, cars stopped, men leapt out; "I know you," they pleaded, "I know you, please." She was followed onto subway platforms.

Her phone was unlisted. She went out for a drink with Tony, flirted with Philip, danced with James, gave her phone number to Kevin, and went home with Mark. She inhaled cocaine off the bathroom sink of the old Gasworks, danced until eleven in the morning. She was the first to wear sweatpants and high heels with a gold chain around her ankle, and she was the first to stop doing that.

Now she was through with all of it. She marked term papers and essays on the codifications of gender and the objectification of women.

"No feelings at all … just hunger."

Her old words straightened him like a jab to the throat.

Sax. Joanna. On her back behind the baseball diamond. Her mouth open. Her teeth shone as though covered in dew. His hand was on her thigh, drifting north. "I'm wet," she laughed, and removed his hand. Overhead the nighthawks cleaved through the moths, ravenous, bleating for them. They were not really hawks, Hessler knew that. A different family. He didn't know what family. They ripped the night like knives.

Jackman, Steve …

Sax, Joanna …

The names swam across the pages, were blotted out, surfaced, sank again. Blackwell, Richard … Hessler had been at his wedding. These days Richard took his empty beer bottles back to the store by cab, his upper body was covered in eczema, he had been implicated in a serious crime and quite possibly his phone was tapped. Once they had climbed mountains together and contracted colds from the same woman.

He turned over a full page of travel agencies, bus terminals, and train stations: he saw that his handwriting was a hasty and erratic smear, as if he'd had no time to finish any of it, no time to tear himself from his thrilling life. His teeth were grinding. Where was that life now, he wondered, that thrilling life where the eagles stared into your eyes, and the woman, always the woman, stood alone at the end of the room, bathed by a single spotlight?

Hessler looked up and saw the snow beating against the night.

The Story I Would Write

I WRITE AD copy for Tillman, Cartier & Hoswitch, but really I'm a writer. Put two drinks in me and I'm very much a writer. Throw in a good-looking, dark-haired woman in her late twenties and I'm one of the greatest writers who ever lived.

In order to be a writer you need something to say. This is what I'm explaining to Elizabeth Anne; the dark-haired woman in her late twenties who answers the phone for Tillman, Cartier & Hoswitch. She looks straight back and nods at me. She has a way of doing that.

I get pretty expressive with my hands sometimes, whether I'm drinking or not, and now I notice they're waving in front of me like pigeons. "Without something to say"— I'm about to tell Elizabeth Anne that without something to say you might as well write ad copy for Tillman, Cartier & Hoswitch. Only the thing is I *do* write ad copy for Tillman, Cartier & Hoswitch. So I stop. There's a silence.

Behind us someone starts banging out "Chopsticks" on the lounge piano. At the next table a group of women are drinking too much and starting to yell at each other.

People. I change my track here. You've got to have something to say about people. What could sound more callow than that? Just the thing a writer says to a good-looking woman after he's got a few drinks in him. The truth is I don't even like people. I don't go out of my way to like them.

You've got to write about people, everybody knows that. I'm trying to regroup here. That's another thing about Elizabeth Anne, not only does she have the eyes, she's patient. She's got the grace to sit there and wait for me to regroup.

"I think you're right," she says carefully, and it sounds like she's given the matter some serious thought.

At the next table those four women have drunk themselves into the maudlin phase: "I told her if she dies of cancer I will not feel one ounce of sorrow. I told her that. That's exactly what I said. I put my face right up to her and said, 'You die of cancer and you'll have no one to blame but yourself.'" The woman rubs her hands together and at that point I look away.

People. You've got to write about people. But it's more than that, and this is what I'm trying to get across to Elizabeth Anne. It's not just people. It's what *happens* to them. Take you, for example. I piece together the little bits I know about her; last name is Racicot: what could be more Quebecois than Racicot? But it turns out Elizabeth Anne Racicot was born in Thunder Bay, to a nautical engineer and a nurse from County Sligo; they fell in love right here at this very bar, drinking Manhattans at the Silver Rail on Yonge Street in Toronto, gave birth to two daughters, one's Elizabeth Anne; the other lives in Edmonton, in a rooming house with the curtains closed because her no-good boyfriend moved out to Vancouver, and she's gone a bit strange over that.

Out the window the street's packed with people marching back and forth. So many people out there it makes me wonder what they're for exactly. But the thing is — I try to make this clear to Elizabeth Anne — whether you like people or not, every one of them has a story. That sounds stupid too. Like saying everyone's got a novel inside them. Maybe they do. Only how many people are smart enough to leave it in there, where it belongs?

It becomes clear that one of the women next to us has some dirt on the brother-in-law of someone's ex-husband and she's dying to spill it.

"I've never told a soul about this," she says as loud as she can. "But do you know what that man did?" I'm not listening. I refuse to let myself get sidetracked by what people say when they've had too much to drink.

"The thing is, with people ... I mean ... you look out the window, you see this parade of human beings. Like that guy there, with the paper bag under his arm. He looks like nobody. Right?"

Elizabeth Anne nods.

"Except that sixteen years ago his wife left him for a golf pro, so now he's taking a veal sandwich home with him in a paper bag, and he's feeling ashamed of that. He's part of that generation of men who never learned to cook except to burn toast and fry eggs. There he is, he's sixty-eight years old, he's got a warmed-up veal sandwich in a paper bag under his arm, and he's slightly ashamed of it. All the big schemes he had about the world are gone. He gets into the elevator where he lives, fifteenth floor, and he's hoping he's the only person in there. He doesn't want that veal sandwich smelling up the elevator and letting people know he's just someone coming home with

a sandwich under his arm because his wife left him for someone else."

I see Elizabeth Anne's still following me. She nods, so I go on.

"The thing is that forty years ago this same guy's dug into the
Pusan Perimeter in North Korea. Nineteen years old. Shells
are going off all around him. Men are getting killed. His best
friend's in the next foxhole with a steel fragment the size of a
baseball wedged in his stomach, and he's screaming out the
guy's name. What can you do, that kid's dead already, he just
doesn't know it yet. They're both teenagers, volunteered on a
dare after getting drunk at a football game in Varsity Stadium.
Thought it would be a laugh. Now people are shooting at him,
it's minus five with snow on the ground and bombs going off.
Guys are running like hell out of there. That kid's frozen up, he's
in tears. Finally he gets captured and spends the next two years
in a prison camp in North Korea getting his face slapped and
having kiln lime thrown on him."

My hands are flying around in front of me again, like birds. I
watch them settle on a sleeve of dark ale, and I take a pull from
it. Elizabeth Anne does the same. She doesn't say anything. Just
takes a short draw from her glass and puts it down very steadily
on the table.

Next to us those four women have evaporated into a mist of
cigarette smoke. They're still jabbering, but I can't hear much
of it; just a few mouths moving up and down. Elizabeth Anne
looks as though she's going to say something, but doesn't.
She's the shy type, which is fine by me. My wife's the opposite;
she's got a Ph.D. in linguistics so I barely get a word in edgewise.
With her it's all phonemes and anemones.

I try to get back on track by explaining to Elizabeth Anne

about the story I'd write; how it would tell every remarkable, unbelievable thing that happens to us whether we want it to or not. Like that old man over there, for example, doing the cryptic crossword puzzle in *The Globe and Mail*. Turns out he was sent up north in 1953 by the Department of Northern Affairs to give names to Eskimos. They were doing a census, and this guy's job was to go up to Pangnirtung and stencil numbers on people's arms. He takes some Inuk aside and he stencils E-2-2 on his forearm. E-2-2. So then you get a whole lineage of people called Eetootoo. You've got Johnny Eetootoo, and Sally Eetootoo. Look at him. He's over there warming a double vermouth and doing a crossword.

I'm starting to heat up now. I take a deep look at Elizabeth Anne and realize her eyes are not so much limpid blue as they are cerulean. Suddenly all the memories that fall off a person's life are piling up in front of me. That's what I'm trying to get across to her; how that inconsequential old lady crocheting doilies for her daughter's armoire, at one time watched a seven-hundred-pound polar bear climb into a rowboat with her and her father while fishing char on a lake in Labrador in 1933. Her father drove a gaff into its eye and made it go away. Later on a vacation to see tulips in Ottawa, she spent fourteen hours in a train berth making love to a traveller in commercial farm engines she met in the dining car while spreading jam on a piece of toast. She was twenty-two.

The hard part always is to find some sort of structure so you can hold a story like that together. Sometimes I think about it when I'm at work. I've got the boards for a new assignment on the desk in front of me; BRAND NAMES AT DISCOUNTED PRICES: *It's worth a boo!* but my mind's somewhere else; I'm thinking about Wendy Richter, and the room we lived in twenty years ago on Elgin Street, the morning she took in a stray cat that showed up on the window ledge, and had four consecutive litters in that little room because neither of us had the money to get it fixed. I'm wondering how to work that in with the terrified kid in a foxhole in the Pusan, or the night Wendy Richter lay beside me on a foam mattress held up by four Sealtest crates, and was concerned about her mother. She had just discovered that her mother's old freezer was packed with dead animals. Every squirrel, every gopher the woman had ever hit with a car, every songbird, every dead cat she had ever brought in, was in there, wrapped in a plastic bag and lying frozen stiff in her basement freezer. She was worried about her mother, and then a month later Wendy was killed. Two mechanics taking an aluminum bass boat under the bridge at Kichi Bay, on the Madawaska River, struck her in the base of the skull while she was swimming. I was playing pinball in a convenience store in west Toronto when it happened.

I'd like to get all that down on a sheet of paper, but it doesn't seem possible. Here I am drinking beer with Elizabeth Anne Racicot in a bar on Yonge Street in Toronto. Thirty years ago her parents sat holding hands and falling in love, right here, in these same two chairs maybe.

Across from us the four women are arguing about Jamaican roti. The one says the best roti in the city's made by a woman named Stella who runs a takeout place on Bathurst, next door to her therapist's office. Her friend says forget it, the best roti comes from a West Indian stall in Kensington Market. I'm thinking about my wife. She's at home watching television. When she's not doing post-doctoral research in linguistics, she watches television. She'd like to have a baby. We haven't slept together in three months so it's not looking good in that regard.

I look over at Elizabeth Anne and see her eyes and an arrow of pale skin beneath her throat. She looks at me and sees me looking at her, then looks away. Outside, the lilting Doppler effect of a siren surges up and away like a trombone. An ambulance crowds into the traffic. There's so much going on I can't even see it all, let alone hold it together for a story. For now, a little bit of it has gathered in the Silver Rail with a woman who works for an ad agency called Tillman, Cartier & Hoswitch, but really should be called Tillman & Hoswitch because Cartier is in a coma after drinking three cocktails and putting his car into a guardrail. The story sits as plain as one of those pretzels the waitress brought for us; perfectly formed, with every grain of salt still on it. All I have to do is get up, go home, and write the thing down exactly the way it is in my head. Only just then the waitress comes over and says,

"Would you like another drink?"

As a matter of fact I would like another drink. It turns out that Elizabeth Anne would like another drink, too.

So we sit there without saying a word, waiting for the next round to come.

Out West

SHE WAS A tall, wide-hipped woman from Uranium City, Saskatchewan and she came straight at me. Her name was Valerie, she wore a purple top purchased from a market in Tel Aviv and a belt made by a man who crafted leather for a living and who tried to marry her, but failed. Her hair was red, two beads of sweat shone between her breasts, her toenails were green, and the third toe on her left foot had a ring on it. Her eyes were blue, and when she laughed it sounded like a trout stream that still had trout in it.

I met her at a conference for the parents of children with early onset autism, spina bifida, and the other diseases that afflict children. I was there because of Tommy, who is six years old and can't hold his head straight. When he's happy he makes a sound like an owl and when he's not he slaps his face. She was something of an expert on children with problems; that's why she was there. I was there because a psychiatrist said it would be good for me.

You expect at a conference like that people will talk incessantly about dystonia, meningitis, muscular dystrophy, and how having a child who may never go to the bathroom by himself will affect your marriage. But mostly what we did was drink. We drank vodka coolers. We drank Italian wine and Portuguese wine. We drank Tanqueray, tequila, Tia Maria, and Zinfandel, and we drank beer, Valerie in particular drank beer. She drank a dark, potent prairie brew called Haymaker, and she drank a lot of it. She called herself an "alpha female." She loved chocolate, classical music, children's literature, word games, low-cut sleeveless tops that showed her breasts, and for some reason she liked me. Her first husband had died in a tractor-trailer accident on the Trans-Canada. Her second husband played bass guitar for a house band in a Regina bar, and she refused to go there for fear she would punch his face, destroy his drum kit and be brought up on charges, like the last time. Her current husband (she called him a "pseudo-husband") seemed to exist in the backrooms of her house, and I got the impression he would not be doing even that for very much longer. At the age of sixteen she had had flesh surgically removed from her thighs in the belief they were unsightly. "My pre-feminist days," she laughed, and glanced down at her beer bottle to a place that seemed to be far away and packed with secrets.

When she wasn't looking I'd stare at her. I had wanted to forget that women could look like that. I looked at her and remembered the first time I saw my wife twenty years ago. She was barefoot, wearing jeans and a T-shirt, walking in broad daylight across the commons area of Trent University. She had on a pair of enormous sunglasses and a book by Simone de Beauvoir under her arm, and she was smoking a cigarette.

THE FIRST DAY we wore name tags but the tags came off quickly. We attended seminars on grief, anger, acceptance, and how to repair wheelchairs. We mixed, we socialized, we exchanged business cards, we stood up at lecterns and said, "Hello, my name's Mr. Smith and I'm the father of a special needs child." Mostly I sat in the back and left early. I did not stand up at the lectern. I was afraid that if I got up there I'd say, "Hello, my name's Mr. Smith and I'm the father of a boy who is irreversibly retarded." I'd tell them how when I see Tommy on the floor in the play room where we've laid the extra matting, my heart turns to stone.

In the evening we assembled in the lounge and spilled out onto the lawn holding our drinks and laughing too loudly. I sat beside Valerie on a bench. The northern lights were out but she was unimpressed by that. She lived in Edmonton now and unless the lights were red and green and twisting like a dragon, she had no time for them. I told her I'd seen a coyote in Toronto, drinking from a public water fountain, but she was unimpressed by that too. She lived in a townhouse on the outskirts of Edmonton, and a coyote family had set up a den beneath the building. The pups kept her awake at night.

There was nothing I could do to compete with her. She had been chased by a bear and shot at by a farmer's wife. She had taught dyslexic children to read, published three books, and was about to embark on a tour of the northwestern reserves of Alberta, collecting oral histories of Assiniboine women.

She sought me out in the cafeteria, holding a tray and looking around with her immense eyes, and then plopped her dinner tray down beside me. "Hi, bud," she said, "how are you?" She ate like a wolf, smacked her lips, wiped her mouth with the back of her bare arm, and went for seconds.

On the last night we got drunk. There was dancing. I felt

better about having a child who was irreversibly retarded. I felt better about a lot of things. When I danced with Valerie she pulled up tight so her chest was pressed against me. She was humming, her eyes were closed and she was happy in that place that women go to when they've had some drinks, and their husbands are far away, and Van Morrison is playing on the stereo.

Later we sat at that same bench outside. I told her I was glad to be there, and glad to meet her. "Good," she said. "Me too." She told me Toronto was a dump. Edmonton was the place. In Edmonton they had opera that made you cry.

At one point she let her head roll to one side so it rested on my shoulder. Her eyes were closed. When she opened them she didn't seem to know where she was. Later I walked her to her room and we kissed each other, half on the lips and half off, and that was that.

NEXT MORNING I packed up my suitcase and drove home. It took three hours. Rachel was in the kitchen making a salad and chopping a banana into pieces so that Tommy could eat it. She had read on the Internet about gluten and children with autism, and was giving it a try. She was game to try anything.

"Hi," she offered.

"Hello," I said. Neither of us raised our voices anymore. Sometimes we barely whispered.

"Did it go all right?

"It went good. It didn't go bad. How did it go here?"

"Oh, here it went pretty well."

That was how we talked to each other. She had forgiven me for the failure of my seed, and I had forgiven her. Together we had forgiven our chromosomes, or the mercury, the Freons, the pcbs, the exhaust fumes, all of it. She had even forgiven God.

"Where's Tommy?" I said this as if Tommy might have just gone skateboarding to the library. There was really only one place Tommy could be: the room that used to be the dining room, but now was Tommy's room.

I went into it and Tommy was there lying on the floor with a bicycle helmet on his head. He seemed not to hear me walking down the hall or entering the room. If he did hear me he didn't move or turn his head, or look in my direction, or make any indication that I was standing next to him. I've been told that there is a good chance Tommy hears me, but the message is scrambled and doesn't make any sense to him. He *smells* my footsteps instead of hears them. Maybe they smell to him like the colour yellow, so he starts to think about bananas and how he might like to eat one. None of this gives him any reason to turn around and look at me.

I put my hand on his shoulder and he felt the way he should; my son, a boy of six with a body that was as warm as blood and scented like milk. He had the form of an angel. My son took my touch without surprise, as if he had been lying there expecting it.

"Aahh," he said finally. Aahh was the first word he ever spoke. He was nineteen months old at the time. It was the second word he spoke as well. By then he was three. At four he made a sound that Rachel interpreted as "momma" but to me it had sounded like "wow-wa-a." Lately when he was very excited he made a sound like, Yee, yeee, yee-ah, yeee ... Then he would smile and toss his head from one side to another.

That night me and Rachel lay together in bed upstairs like

we always did. She talked to me with her silence, I answered back with my breath. There was a mole on her left shoulder that had been a mark of beauty to me. Now it was just a mole; a mark of daily things, of coffee that we made each other in the morning and of the feelings that we still had for each other. I stroked the mole on her back, she sighed. Then silence.

I fell asleep and dreamt at once of a beautiful golden boy with his knees up and his hands crossed at the chest. A man, me I think, was pouring sand over him. The sand was tumbling down onto his face, into his mouth, drifting in dunes over his body, and then I woke up.

In the morning I left my office and crossed the factory floor with the drawings. I'd drawn them up the night before; a simple basic design for a ribbed steel basket, like the ones the newspaper carriers used to bolt to the front of their bicycles; a steel grid sturdy enough to hold fifty Saturday papers with the funnies and the flyers and everything. The welder looked at the sketch and nodded. His name was Mike Staunton; he was the father of two boys who played soccer, one of them well enough to get his picture in the paper.

"Yeah, that's not a problem," he said. By four o'clock he had it done.

THE NEXT MORNING it was Saturday and Rachel was out at the group that she attended on Saturdays. It was made up of people like us who had children with autism, or spina bifida, or muscular dystrophy. They sat together in a room with a potted jade tree and discussed pervasive development disorders, or the pros and cons of applied behavioural analysis. One of the women there was saving money to put her daughter into a tank with a dolphin. At first Rachel came back from these meetings excited, and with names written down in a little notebook: a doctor at UCLA, a physiotherapist at Mount Sinai who had published a paper. Lately she had stopped coming back with names.

While she was out I fastened the carrier to my mountain bike. I had the supports bolted into the front axle when Tommy came out and took a long look at what I was doing. He held a piece of yellow string and occasionally looked down at it, then up at me, with alarm.

"It's okay, kid, it's okay." Tommy contorted himself, glanced down at his feet, then dropped the string.

Rachel came in at about noon with two plastic bags stuffed with groceries. We ate lunch. Tommy kept flattening a cube of squash with his thumb, but finally was persuaded to eat several pieces of banana and four yellow beans. For some reason he only ate food that was yellow. Finally he lost interest and slumped against the chair.

"It's all right, you don't have to sit here, you can go play." Rachel nodded at him. Tommy made a face then slid off his chair and left the room, angling sideways to the door.

"He's not eating enough."

"He's fine," I said.

She sighed; I pretended not to hear her.

"I'm taking him for a ride," I said suddenly, almost angrily.

"What do you mean?"

"A bicycle ride. I had a carrier made; Mike, at work. Mike Staunton, the welder. He made it for me. I'm taking Tommy for a ride."

Rachel looked at me as if to say something, but didn't. She had always wanted this, for *my* sake she thought, not hers: for me to get down the baseball glove from the top of the closet and toss a ball back and forth, to explain to him the points of how to yield when the ball comes to you on a hop, to give in to it, to embrace it, "soft hands, kid, soft hands." She had wanted all the things it was possible to want; the silent, steady bond she thought should exist between a father and her son.

"Good," she said doubtfully. "He'll like that."

But Tommy didn't like it at all. He didn't like that I had my arms around his chest and was lifting him off the ground. He attempted what his physical therapist calls a "body drop," where he throws his weight flat against the floor so you can't get your hands underneath to lift him. The tactic has left Rachel in tears in supermarkets, with people glaring at her. I was expecting it and got my palms underneath him in time, and managed to lower him feet first into the carriage. Tommy had already adjusted his legs to prevent his feet from going through and hung there cross-legged, like a Buddha, confused, and staring abjectly out the garage as if some help was coming. Finally I swung myself over the saddle, clasped him by the ankles and pushed his legs down between the grid, one on each side of the wheel.

"Here we go, kid."

From the garage I got a rolling start. At once Tommy arced his back, stiffening his legs as I pedalled west to the edge of the hill. The sun was in front of me, red and almost heatless. I pedalled past the MacIntyres' and the Wilburtons', and Shelley Nicholson, who stood on her front lawn with a green garden hose at her feet, spraying a prismatic halo of water into the air. I waved to her but she was caught up in her own thoughts and did not see me. I pedalled past the high school that Tommy will not be allowed to go to, and saw the kids shooting hoops, slicing toward the basket with their swift, perfect bodies.

Then I was to the hill, on the slant with the willows and the goldenrod whipping faster and faster past the corners of my eyes. The air slapped Tommy in the face and he leaned back, cringing from it.

"Yaa eee," he hollered, as the wind spread tears from the corner of his eyes. I stopped pedalling. "Yaaa eee!" Tommy screamed at the top of his lungs now.

From nowhere I screamed back at him. Tommy had never heard me do that before. He had never thought that he could scream into the darkness, or the light, or whatever it is that he sees, and that exact same sound would come back out of it. At once he twisted his neck to look at me; his eyes enormous, and unblinking.

"Ya aaa-eee," he tried again, louder this time, and smiled.

"Ya aaa-eee," I answered, and Tommy tossed his head from one side to the other, grinning and screaming as we flew down the hill.

The People
Behind the Hedge

WHEN MY WIFE left me for the second time and I was undergoing court-ordered anger-management sessions at a clinic in the city, I would walk around the streets and stare at the buildings — the darkened buildings made of brick with crenellated rooftops and steamed-up windows from the coffee shops and restaurants that took up the street level. I was killing time, really. I had not had a drink in twenty-seven days, although I sensed those drinks were heading my way, like mail that hadn't made it through the slot yet. I walked back and forth and wondered what people did behind those steamed-up windows and dark bricks, what went on in their minds.

I found myself standing in front of a dark square building with a sign on it: *Wentworth County Museum*. The door was open and I went in, dropping two dollars into a donation jar that was carefully guarded by two elderly women who sat behind a table, knitting. The room was poorly lit. I smelled the old odours from my childhood; musty newspapers now mounds of fungus, the things made of wood, butter churns, and old horse harnesses dried to the texture of punk. On one wall hung century-old daguerreotypes of the town I had grown up in; the men wearing hats, a lone dispirited horse, the mud streets and the plank sidewalks by the library that had been built with Andrew Carnegie's tainted money and at one time seemed to grace every small town in Canada. In a glass display case stood a collection of raggedy dolls with bonnets on their heads, and behind them toy wagons carved out of wood, harnessed with string or wool.

The rest of the museum was filled with photographs and mimeographed correspondence, and on one wall hung an enormous handmade banner:

THEY CAME THROUGH SLAUGHTER

THE LIFE OF COLONEL ARTHUR STINTSON

SOLDIER AND BAND LEADER

Every letter had been carefully scissored from black poster paper, probably by the same two volunteers who had met me at the door. I began to look at the pictures and the first photograph I stood in front of showed Colonel Arthur Stintson. He wore a khaki uniform packed with so many medals that he appeared to be sagging from the weight of them. Prime Minister Diefenbaker, sporting enormous jowls, was shaking his hand and, except for the uniform and the medals, he looked exactly the way he did when I had known him, thirty-eight years earlier.

I WAS SIX years old then and I played in a large backyard that had a chestnut tree and a tall hedge instead of a fence. The hedge was thick and trimmed, but I managed to force my way through it, pretending I was a soldier on a battlefield, sneaking up on the enemy to kill him. Exactly how I would do this was not clear; probably I would say "Bang," and the man would fall down and be dead.

On the other side of that hedge I was greeted, somewhat warily, by two old people. To me they seemed very old. They were both bone white; their hair was white and their clothes were white; the man wore white trousers cinched with a white belt and sat in a white wicker chair beneath a white trellis. I was astonished to see that the hairs on his arm were white, too, and his skin was white, except for the many brown spots, the size of pennies, that dotted his arms and hands. Hers as well. The yard was green and thick with white flowers in blossom. Everything in that yard was in blossom.

They were the Stintsons, Mr. and Mrs. I knew this. They were not very surprised to see a small boy emerge from the hedge, and make his way toward them. They were not exactly pleased to see me, but they were not surprised. After several moments, Mrs. Stintson got up and went slowly into the house and came back with lemonade in a tall glass that she placed on the white table alongside the two teacups. Probably she expected me to sip my lemonade over the course of the afternoon, but instead I grabbed the glass with both hands, poured it down my throat, handed the glass back, and burped. I was eager to show them that I could burp whenever I wanted to. This did not impress them. In fact, Mrs. Stintson told me I shouldn't do that. The crudities of boys made her wince but she never once ordered me from the yard or told me not to come back.

I began to push my way through that hedge every day, sometimes twice a day. My mother was intrigued by these comings and goings of mine. She believed naturally enough that any child of hers was an enormous gift to the world, and that the world ought to be hugely grateful to have me. Maybe a small part of her thought that by allowing me to crawl through the hedge and visit those two old and, in her estimation, lonely people, she was doing them a favour. She was also glad to get me out of her hair for a few moments. If she'd seen the way I carried on with them, probably she would have yanked me out of there in a hurry and slapped me.

I came to the Stintsons like a stray cat in the afternoon and they tolerated me. I tried to get Mr. Stintson to rise out of his chair and chase me. But Mr. Stintson got out of his chair for no one. He was extremely old and I had no idea what it meant to be that; the chill in the extremities, or the sudden pain that stabs the ribs, and leaves you breathless and sweating. Even though she was a woman, I tried to get Mrs. Stintson to play Cowboys and Indians with me. The game was simple; all she had to do was watch me while I demonstrated new and acrobatic ways to fall off my horse and die. But she did not want to have anything to do with Cowboys and Indians. Instead she stood beside Mr. Stintson and served him tea and white cakes that he never touched. In the end it was me who ate them all, pushing them into my mouth one after another, as if I was afraid they would demand them back.

"You mustn't do that," she said, and I thought she meant that I mustn't shove all the cakes into my mouth. But she meant Cowboys and Indians. I mustn't play that game, or even put those words together in the same sentence, not in front of Mr. Stintson who sat in his white chair straining forward as if to put a stop to something that was taking place just out of his reach. His white fingers gripped the knees of his trousers and he stared at the hedge, his mouth forming words that would not come to him. "You must try to be peaceful," said Mrs. Stintson. It seemed she was saying this to the both of us, to the whole world even.

AT DINNER I told my parents the news about how I was not allowed to play Cowboys and Indians in front of Mr. Stintson.

"It's because he fought with them," my father said.

"He fought with them?" I stared at him and imagined a black and white Hollywood movie with Mr. Stintson going hand-to-hand with an Apache Indian, both of them rolling among the tumbleweeds with their knives out and flashing, while the redskin made a terrifying ululating noise from his throat, the way they did on the TV.

"Not against them. *With* them. That's what I said. In the war. He fought with them. With Indians."

"Did you?" I tried.

I knew my father had fought in the war because my mother had told me. "Never mind your father," she would say, "it's because of the war." Later she dropped the war part altogether and said only, "Never mind your father." I had discovered that my father kept his war medals in the bottom drawer of his dresser beneath his socks and a magazine that had pictures of naked ladies in it. My father looked up from his plate and glared at me.

"Not *that* war." He stared at me strangely for a moment. "The first one," he said, and went back to his dinner.

THE FOLLOWING SUMMER the visits to the old people who lived behind the hedge came to an end. My father drove his car over a bridge and landed it in the creek where the smelt ran, along with a tree branch and a length of railing. The police came to our home. They came again on a different matter, but my mother wouldn't tell me what it was. Then my mother and father stopped speaking to each other and after that they stopped living in the same house. I moved with my mother to an apartment in a duplex that smelled of fried onions and looked out on the cemetery. She took up smoking again and every second week my father came. I got in the car with him, and we went for a drive in the country where I saw the cows and the apple trees lined up in rows, like soldiers.

I sat beside my father and asked him about the war. What had he done in it? This mattered to me more than anything. All I knew, or thought I knew, was that one dreadful night while standing waist deep in water he had seen the corpse of a woman floating in front of him, and when he poked at it with his rifle to keep it off him, the corpse had separated into pieces. My mother told me this story after he had hit her. He hit her and then he left the house slamming doors and gunning the car out of the driveway. She was sitting at the kitchen table with ice cubes wrapped in a dishtowel pressed to the side of her face when she told me this story. "You have to forgive your father," she said. It was the war. Things happened to him there.

But in the car when I asked my dad what had happened to him in the war he said nothing; he just pressed his jaws together as if driving an automobile required a man to do that.

"You want to know what I did in the war? I'll tell you. I was a hero. I killed the cook. Shot him between the eyes and blew his brains out." He grinned. "The guys gave me a medal for it."

It was the oldest war joke in the world, but it was not funny to me. I sat next to him frustrated by his refusal to tell me what I wanted to know. I wanted to know his heroism, I wanted to know what it looked like and what it would look like for me when I grew up and became a hero, just like him. "Tell me," I insisted.

His mood changed at once and he wiped his fist across his lips. "You keep your mouth shut," he said.

NEARLY FORTY YEARS later I stood in the Wentworth County Museum moving slowly from wall to wall, reading every caption. I learned that for most of his life Mr. Stintson had been the conductor of a brass band made up of young Native men off the Six Nations reserve. Their faces were there in front of me, posed artificially; stern, dark, handsome faces, propped up by high-necked uniforms that gave way to lean and fit bodies with horns instead of rifles pressed to their shoulders. In front of me were Cayugans who played the clarinet, a Mohawk with a tuba wrapped around him. I saw them assembled in the outdoor lacrosse rinks at Oshweken and the drill halls of small-town armouries, or assembled in the band shells of the towns on the banks of the Grand River. In many of the photos they had been dressed up in the ornate feathery gear of the Plains Indians, even though most of them were Six Nations from Brantford, Ontario and welded high steel for a living. Mr. Stintson himself was dressed up that way and looked more ashamed than the rest of them. Later, these young men had taken off those tacky Hiawatha Festival costumes and boarded troop ships that took them to the Somme, Ypres, the Marne, Vimy Ridge, Amiens, and Passchendaele.

In most of the photographs, Mr. Stintson was unrecogniz-able in his youth. In others, a stunning dark-haired woman pressed against him, wrapped in a brilliant full-length squirrel coat with her ankles showing underneath and her hair piled up, in thick and gleaming coils. That was her, the old lady in white with the penny-sized age spots on her hands, who had given me no end of lemonade and tried to explain to me that I had to be peaceful, that I could not play Cowboys and Indians in front of her husband.

For two hours I read the text pasted beneath those photographs. I read his war letters and his love letters; the words that a man composes to a woman when he is young and nothing has gone wrong between them yet. I read his poetry, and the diary entries, the scattering of words that he wrote to himself in his solitude and his horror: *I watched Private Winston Longboat go into the mud. One boot stayed out longer than the other. Then it was gone too.* A framed fragment of a poem written in pencil, several lines meant for his wife, and never sent:

> *What is left of my faith is this blister,*
> *what is left of my soul is this blister.*

When I reached the end of the display I sat down in a red upholstered chair. Probably I was not supposed to sit in it at all. It had the look of a severe, high-backed parliamentary chair from which some important legislation had passed into law; a museum piece. But I sat down in it anyway, and tried to breathe. I could not shake an image of mud sliding into the mouths of those men from the Six Nations. It was as if their brass instruments had been detached from their lips and replaced by mud. I thought of my father when things were falling apart for him, and my mother holding the ice to the side of her face. At the time I had wanted to hit him with my own little hands. Once again I saw the look in my wife's eyes when she lifted her arms, afraid that I would strike her, and then backed away from me in the room of a house that the courts have taken away from me. I remembered Mr. Stintson all those years ago in his yard, when he seemed to be responding to a spasm in his back, reaching out to do something he couldn't, as if he was trying to grab the exposed boots and the curled fingers of all the men he couldn't save.

I sat in that heavy red chair and I tried to reach for the hands of all those men, too; the clarinet player from Cayuga and his brother who played the French horn. I wanted to wade into the ocean beside my father and block his view so he would not face the woman with the swollen body who floated to him. I saw myself reach out to remove the ice pack from the side of my mother's face, and finally I touched my wife's hair to soothe her, and to let her know she would never have to be afraid of me again.

Innocent

CHRISTOPHER STOOD IN his bedroom furious and even ashamed of himself. He needed to go back downstairs at once and apologize to his wife. He needed to console her and put his arms around her and make up. Instead he sat down on the bed, breathing heavily, with the weight of his anger thudding inside him.

Down the hall he heard his daughters whispering cautiously to each other before shutting their bedroom door. He had reduced his daughters to whispers. His wife was downstairs sobbing; doors were shutting on him that would not open again. This was *his* fault and it was unbearable to him and he turned at once toward the door and was through it, taking the stairs two at a time.

Madeleine stood in the same spot where he had left her, by the sink with her hands on the counter. Her wedding ring looked large and gaudy to him but she was no longer crying; she was stone-faced and withdrawn.

"Maddy," he said. Now that she was in front of him he could not find the proper words to bring himself to her. He could not apologize with the sincerity he had a felt a moment ago. He was getting angry all over again. It was the anger of his innocence. His wife did not recognize his innocence and this infuriated him. He wanted it acknowledged right now, this moment, in this kitchen, and he wanted it acknowledged not only by her but by his daughters who remained upstairs whispering behind closed doors as if to protect themselves from a criminal.

I am not a criminal, he thought, though in fact he must have spoken this, for Madeleine said to him, flatly, at once, "I never said you were a criminal."

"What?" he demanded.

"I never said you were a criminal." She spoke matter-of-factly, as she always did, indifferently even, and Christopher realized he was angry with her all over again.

"I'm sick of being blamed. Do you hear me?" But she did not hear him at all. She had exited the room at the first rising of his voice and Christopher realized he was now standing in the kitchen by himself. "What do you want from me?" he shouted after her, aware that he sounded ridiculous.

He stood frustrated and trembling. How had everything gone this wrong so quickly? His chest beat like a valve and he knew that a decisive act was required of him; a gesture so dramatic it would leave no doubt about his innocence. Go out for a drink, he thought, and pondered what it meant to do that. He had not gone "out for a drink" since his campus years, and even then the phrase itself had sounded pitiable to him, like a military tactic that was doomed to failure. Regardless, he went into the hall and put on a light jacket and left the house, allowing the door to slam loud enough behind him so that the household could feel his conviction and the weight of his innocence.

OUTSIDE THE AIR was neither cold, nor warm; it was hardly anything. The sky behind the church was about to go dark, but just as easily it could have been the pre-dawn, getting ready for daylight. The soles of his shoes scratched the concrete. On the corner the old Arlington Hotel leaned into the night but he did not go into it. It was not his sort of place. The windows were painted black and the grubby yellow light fixtures above the door gave off the air of a sailors' bar, even though Christopher knew there were no sailors in the city. He passed a neon Irish establishment called *O'Gradyhans*, a name he found too desperately Irish to be believable, and did not enter the place. He was alarmed not only by the name but by the total exposure of the front window and the high stools on which the customers were forced to perch themselves. Christopher had never realized just how many places there were for a man to go out and have a drink.

He stopped in front of a door that was familiar to him; the Saville Restaurant and Bar. He'd been here before for dinner and lunch, him and Maddy and the girls, several years ago when his daughters were effectively children and were still talking to him without reserve. At that time the Saville Restaurant and Bar had just been the Saville Family Restaurant.

He entered confidently, even forcefully, which proved a mistake, for the Saville Restaurant and Bar was crowded with customers standing together, laughing and curling their shoulders protectively over their drinks. Everyone was talking much louder than was needed.

"Hey," cried someone from behind the door, "watch what you're doing, asshole." The stranger made a gesture as if to punch Christopher in the shoulder but shook his head at him instead, vigorously.

"Sorry," said Christopher, immediately. "I didn't know you were there." The young man continued to shake his head, either in anger, or in time to the music that pulsed from speakers in the corners. A Chinese ideogram showed on the front of his black toque and two sideburns crawled out from beneath it. The man stood with his fists hanging at his sides, grinning, leering even, in a way that Christopher found difficult to interpret. His two friends looked on, dressed the same way, in brimless black wool hats. One of them had silver studs glinting from his face. Christopher realized they were the sort of young men his daughters would soon be bringing home and falling in love with. This demoralized him physically, in the region of his stomach.

It was best to have done with this crowd, he knew that, and pushed on to the bar. Before he was out of range he felt a knock between his shoulders, a tap or even a light punch with the bottom palm of a fist. Even though he commanded himself not to look back, his indignation overcame him and he swivelled and glanced around to where the blow had originated. He saw the three young men there, as identical as crows.

"I'm sorry," said the tallest one, in a screeching mimicry of Christopher's voice, "I didn't know you were there." His companions found this remark unspeakably funny and convulsed into laughter which, to Christopher's surprise, was joined, even surpassed, by the chimes of a young woman who appeared from behind them, as if she had been concealed in their wings. She could not have been more than five years older than his own eldest daughter, Kathleen. She was piercingly attractive with high-plucked eyebrows and a severe, ultra-stylish slash of black bangs that cut sharply across her forehead. Her lips glowed redder than anything he had ever seen, and he wondered how a young woman of this beauty could end up in the company of such louts.

He reached the bar and sat himself on a padded stool, confident that this was what a man did when he went out for a drink by himself. In the movies this was how it was done, and Christopher took some small pride in that fact that he'd managed to make his life resemble, even a little bit, what people did in the movies. He sat and made his way through a laminated and dizzying list of exotic foreign beers, none of which he recognized. Despite his confusion he managed to arrange for a tall and shapely glass of draft, beaded with clear droplets, to appear on the bar counter that had been cleared and wiped in front of him. He drank it swiftly and another was there and he drank that one as well, feeling for the first time in a month that he had come back to himself. He smiled warmly at the bartender. He shifted his stool generously forward to provide more room for anyone who passed behind him. He would get in the way of no one. He saw men with arms raised in gestures of affectionate backslapping and motions that emphasized goodwill and the fairness of their opinions. Women laughed and hugged each other, even a sleepy dog had been allowed to flop against the far wall. The faces of decent people floated in the room like balloons, and reminded him of murals by that Mexican artist, Diego Rivera, in which the faces of humanity pressed together, so that Christopher now expected a Mexican woman with a sturdy neck to appear at his side and produce a live chicken from beneath a colourful shawl, and offer to sell it to him. "I would buy it, too," he thought, hearing the fragments of the many voices that packed the room.

Halfway through his third glass of beer Christopher knew
that he had reached an apotheosis of generosity. His goodwill
was palpable and he felt he could hold it in his hands like a
warm meat pie just taken out of the oven. He understood now
that he was not innocent at all, not in the way he'd believed
himself to be. In fact he was guilty of a wide range of crimes;
not the least of which was that he had become indifferent to
his wife, and impatient with his children. He was starting
to show disdain toward anyone who was not as smart as him, a
quick resentment toward anyone who, against posted signage,
made a left-hand turn northbound between four and six p.m. on
weekdays. He had insulted and hung up the phone on a quavering
telephone solicitor whose first language was not English and
who, in whatever country he'd fled from, after being tortured
probably, was a respected brain surgeon, and whose only crime,
aside from trying to feed his family, was to ask Christopher
in a friendly voice, "How are you today, sir." His guilt piled
up in front of him like a police rap sheet. It was thicker than
the city phone book. Strangely, he did not feel oppressed by it;
he felt the opposite. His innocence was a fiction, but it was also
an opportunity for him to do better.

He finished his third glass in two quick swallows, paid the
barkeeper, left a tip of three dollars which he calculated to be
generous in the extreme, and pulled his jacket around him
like a new a uniform. It was clear he had to return at once to
his house where the roof did not leak, where the paint on the
walls did not stink of fried onions, and where an alcoholic
divorcee on the floor above him did not spend every afternoon weeping and swearing on the telephone as had happened
in nearly every other shabby ruin that he had lived in prior

to meeting Madeleine. He would put his fingers in her hair and somehow, he would open the doors he had shut on them, and shatter the indifference that had crystallized in the space between their love for each other. Christopher knew that once again he was blessed with a lover's senses. Everything was exalted. The air in the Saville Restaurant and Bar was exalted. The lips of any woman who so much as breathed were exalted. The old sleeping dog in the corner and even the floor beneath it, well scuffed and pitching at a five degree angle, was equally exalted.

Outdoors on the sidewalk he stood beneath stars that could not be seen beyond the clouds and the greyness, and sniffed at the city. It smelled, not unpleasantly, like a grilled hot dog with all the garnishes. At the corner he turned and again passed the black-painted Arlington Hotel. He stood idly for a moment at the entrance to the alley next to it. It looked like the black rectangular space left when a tooth goes missing from a ruined mouth. According to articles that ran in neighbourhood news-papers, things took place in that alley — drugs, and sexual liaisons that involved the handing over of cash, things that brought down the resale value of houses, *his* house. Christopher did not give a damn about that; the resale value of houses meant nothing to him. Only the things that could not be traded or subdivided had any value. He had always known that but somewhere in the blur of years he had forgotten. He would not forget anymore. I will not forget, he thought, and while he was thinking that the back of his right knee exploded and a bullet or a knife or a ball-peen hammer entered the soft crook of his leg and he buckled like a mechanical creature, falling over in the final moments of a low-budget science-fiction film.

Christopher landed hard on his hip and knew he was injured. He became aware of legs, many legs, like black sheaves in a harvest that had produced only black wheat. One of the legs swung toward him like a pendulum of an old grandfather clock, gaining speed as it navigated into his stomach. He was being kicked repeatedly and he knew now that the sound he heard was the heaviest of the blows resonating in the barrel of his chest, sonorous as a drum beat. A boot clipped his face and sent a shower of starlight through his eyes. At once he pulled his arms up to protect his face but the boots seemed to anticipate this, and switched to his exposed midsection. "Stop it," he cried. "Stop it." But no one was listening to him. Nothing stopped; another boot, unique from the others, slammed into the back of his spine and convulsed him. A Chinese ideogram, embroidered in white, floated in front of his eyes, disappeared, and was followed by a vicious kick. This time it was to his midsection, and he knew that he had come apart on the inside. He heard laughter. "Sorry," said the young man. "I didn't know you were there."

Christopher tried to look into the darkness at the people who were doing this to him, but they had him by the legs and dragged him into the unspeakable alley where the unspeakable things took place. Hands were on his body, two sets, like rats running up and down his clothing. He felt his wallet leaving his jacket pocket, joyously, as if it was glad to be gone from him. He smelled stale urine from the alley where all the drunks and all the other desperate people who could not contain themselves went to be relieved. The alley was rank with it. He thought for a moment that the kicking had stopped but he was wrong. He lay on his side gazing up and saw the studs of metal that glinted on the faces. She was there too and this comforted him. Her lips, even in the dark, gleamed intensely red. "You remind me of my daughter," he said to her; at least he hoped he was saying it. He hoped he was speaking to her in a sincere and straightforward manner. It was important that he talk to her in particular; he didn't know why, really.

As he lay there he knew that his two daughters were in the kitchen right now, stirring vegetables in a crock pot. Maddy was helping them make a late dinner. A residue of their fight still hung in the house, but it was fading. The anger was evaporating from the rooms and the hallways. The girls were beginning to soften and make quick jokes with their mother.

Over top of him he saw a look of remote curiosity cross the young woman's face, as if she wanted to see what a man looked like when this was happening to him.

"My eldest daughter will look like you," he said, although he had no reason to believe that she heard him.

Nuptial

MR. HADINE INHALED and took in the breeze. "A perfect day for a wedding," he said. "Even God himself has made a contribution." Mrs. Hadine, who did not approve of God, pressed her teeth together and said nothing.

The guests arrived on time. Some had come great distances by car — from Detroit, and Windsor, Montreal, and upper New York State. "No one comes by train anymore," observed Mr. Hadine, sadly.

More than a few of the guests were pregnant, or writing novels, or both. Percy Salinger was not writing a novel. Instead of writing novels he wrote a column for a city newspaper in which he said nasty things about people he had never met. He had given up on novel writing years ago. "I'm a hack," he liked to say. What he really meant was "*You're* a hack, but you don't have the guts to admit it, the way I do." It was said of Percy Salinger that he had once been slapped in the face by the personal assistant of someone extremely famous.

Next to him stood a cheerful, attractive woman who had undergone an abortion many years ago, and wished now that she hadn't. Weddings made her feel like that.

Next to Percy Salinger and his date stood Angelina Koss and her husband. Mrs. Hadine actually introduced them that way.

"This is Angelina Koss," she announced. "And her husband." His name was not spoken. Nobody seemed to know what it was. He had been in the same line of work for forty years but no one knew what that was. He was pink and bald with liver spots on his head and he had no children, had never raised his voice in anger, made a drunken pass at a woman, or written a novel. When he was nineteen years old he had been tortured for seven days by a screaming North Korean intelligence officer in the Densai Peninsula. He was nearly eighty-nine now and sometimes at night he dreamt that he was back there in the high, cold mountains, and when that happened he woke up crying like a child.

Two women appeared together from the wrong side of the house and were forced to step over a low fence to enter the yard. They both wore colourful, tight dresses and wobbled over the lawn on very tall shoes. The younger of the two wore a five-hundred-dollar hat that gave her the appearance of having arrived directly from the Queen's Plate. Her gums were long and she frequently massaged them with her tongue. Her problems with men were legion.

"This is my date," she laughed and indicated her girlfriend, who laughed with her. Her girlfriend's problems with men were also legion, even more legion than the other's. "Men are weak," she said to anyone who would listen. "I need a man who is strong." Currently she had given herself entirely to a man who owed her forty thousand dollars and was addicted to Quaaludes. He was strong, but he stole cars, gambled in American casinos, stood her up in expensive restaurants and did not return her calls. For the time being even his parole officer did not know his place of residence. "What a perfect day for a wedding," she said.

Wayne Lambert arrived wearing a white cotton shirt, open at the neck, bought specifically for the wedding. His face was pink and knobby, but not unattractive. He held a Ph.D. in statistical analysis and had quietly acquiesced to his wife's demand that they adopt a baby girl. It was not a problem for him. His wife wore a blue dress, spotted white. Her hair hung in ringlets and her novel was at that crucial stage where either it came to fruition or it remained inert, like a slab of meat.

"You hold her." Mrs. Lambert swung their daughter to her husband. The child was nearly five, and long, but Mrs. Lambert insisted on carrying her everywhere. Her husband was afraid that their daughter's limbs were beginning to atrophy; some slackness showed already in the muscles of her bare calves. He received the girl like a package and put her down on the grass at once.

"Wayne!" His wife's voice was high and sibilant, and she glared at him.

"Sorry," he muttered, but it was too late. The girl had touched down, and sat on the ground now in a pink dress that made her look like a pudding. Her mother bent down and swept her from the earth. At once the child began to wail. Her cries were loud and petulant, like a sound made by a carpenter's tool. Several of the guests turned to look.

"See!" Mrs. Lambert bared her teeth at her husband. "See!" She swooped the girl up into the broad, protective circle of her arms. "It's all right, baby, it's all right." No harm would come to her daughter. She stared with a wild intensity at the guests, daring them to think even for one moment that she would allow any harm to come to her daughter. The child seemed to sense this and looked over her mother's shoulders with eyes that were large and pleading.

The woman with Percy Salinger watched. She felt sympathy for the husband. She felt a strange anger towards Mrs. Lambert, but that softened, and she imagined them twelve years from now or less: the little girl who looked like a pudding, in low-slung blue jeans with her underwear flagrantly showing over the top and a tattoo on the small of her back, slapping her fists on the dining room table, shouting "I hate you, I hate what you stand for," fleeing the house into the shade of a tree where a boy was waiting for her.

BY FIVE O'CLOCK all of the guests had arrived and were assembled in knots on the lawn, waiting for someone to take charge. A slender young woman in bare shoulders, with a black brassiere showing above her dress, began to play classical guitar. Percy Salinger slid a chair across the grass and sat close, examining her. His date stood alone on the grass sipping bottled water.

Many of the guests cast about hopefully for wine or beer. But it had been decided by Mrs. Hadine that the wedding would be a spiritual one. "No meat, no God, and no wine," she had proclaimed. Meat made her nauseous, God filled her with rage, and wine turned men into pigs. "No meat, no God, no wine …" She had taken to chanting this into her husband's ear in the moments when they stood together; "No meat, no God, no wine …"

"Shut up," he whispered tensely, but could not stop himself from grinning. Despite his affairs and her daily martyrdom their marriage had lasted forty-three years. It had withstood the death of two of their children; one in a car accident and one at the hands of a surgeon with a drinking problem. They had stood together in the rain at the funeral of their first grandchild who had drowned in a swimming pool. The tops of the pines had rocked in the wind. They had even withstood Mrs. Hadine's hatred of God, which was livid and personal. Children were slaughtered because of God. Abominations, acts of terrorism. Young women stoned to death because of God. Children had their hands cut off because of God. She thought of God as a sexual deviant who molested children and demonstrated this in a lengthy letter to the editors of many newspapers who elected not to publish it.

Her husband had spent seven months in a minimum-security facility at Collingwood for tax evasion. He had made and lost millions, made them back, and lost them again. Ten years ago a young man who was known to the police was walked out on a railway siding near Burlington and shot twice in the face. Whenever this case was revisited in the news, Mr. Hadine's name was obliquely mentioned. While facing a ten-year sentence for conspiracy to commit fraud, he had accepted the Lord Jesus Christ as his saviour, and was acquitted. He prayed frequently and passionately. His hair was pure white and he possessed the lithe, proportioned body of the millionaire who practises yoga.

The groom was stout, with a dense head of silver curls, fifty-five years old, and walked easily among the guests, enfolding them in his large, receptive embrace. They seemed to disappear within him like cars entering a car wash. He knew the names of everyone, including the name of Angelina Koss's husband, whom he wrapped in a long and tender hug, healing him in the places where he had been wounded.

"Philip," he said. "It's so good to see you." He could take a person's pain and place it against his own heart. It was a gift that he had. He looked into people's eyes without causing them to turn away. They felt the generosity of his soul and were unwilling to leave his embrace. He was a loving man. Sometimes his phone rang at three in the morning, his first wife, screaming at him from the dark place of her illness, "You, it's because of you, I'm in here." He would answer the phone, and talk softly until someone at the other end came and took the phone from her.

The bride appeared at last, dressed in a fetching pink wrap, her hair wound in dark coils. She was flanked by two women who were similarly dressed. "Here comes the bride," shouted Percy Salinger, to cheers. A nervous, severe-looking woman of indeterminate age approached the microphone and made an announcement about love. "Love," she explained curtly, "is a unification of the spirit. It is a living union in which two souls become one soul." She went on like that for several minutes, then gold bands were exchanged, then a kiss. A look of gratitude shone from the groom. He had wanted this more than anything; this ritual, public recognition of the two of them together as husband and wife. The bride smiled. "There, you have what you want," she seemed to be saying to him. "I'm no different. I told you it would be this way."

Despite her appearance she was exhilarated and giddy. It was her first marriage. As a little girl there had been a father who used his fists on the children, and a mother who wept and retreated into Valium. At sixteen she was a runaway. There had been men who took her home and kept her there. Men who said they wanted to paint her, but in fact had wanted to do something else. She had eaten cold french fries off the streets of Montreal. For two days she had been kept in a hunting cabin by a man who fed her tinned luncheon meat. There had been sex performed in the rain on crushed cardboard boxes in an alley behind a cinema; money was handed over. Photographs of her had been taken that were on the Internet. Now all of that was behind her, like a tumour cut from her body. She finished a degree in early childhood education, started a job. Suddenly there were men who did not put bruises on her, but took her to Nassau and sent flowers to her office. There were yoga classes, and conferences in Vancouver. Now she was a married woman with a man who loved her more than anyone. A married woman, she told herself.

AFTER DINNER, MRS. HADINE shepherded the guests into a large room in which the carpet had been rolled. Two large speakers were mounted on poles and an eager young man stood between them, flexing his fingers, anxious to start.

"Dance," commanded Mrs. Hadine, pointing Biblically toward the floor. It was understood that under no circumstance would she ever dance herself.

At once the young man went to work; speakers cackled and music boomed from them. The music was loud and from an era that was safely gone. Several women took to the floor in a desultory way. Mrs. Lambert had briefly allowed her daughter's feet to touch the ground, but was careful to shield her from the music by cupping her hands over her ears. She fled the room.

"The baby," she said, in a panic. Her husband followed behind her with an amused and sacrificial air.

The woman who had arrived with Percy Salinger wanted to dance, and looked about the room for him. He was at the table by the soft drinks, nodding intensely to the young classical guitarist with the black brassiere. She saw that he was looking brazenly down the front of her dress and using the loudness of the music as cover to press his lips close to her ear. She took the dance floor by herself. Next to her, the mother of a lovely teenage girl was trying to coax her daughter off the sofa onto the floor, so that people could see how pretty she was.

"Mom!" the girl whispered fiercely. "No!" Her face burned with shame.

"Oh, be like that," sighed the mother and began to dance by herself in the swaying, free-form movements that recalled her own revolutionary youth. Her daughter turned away, mortified by her mother's performance.

Then the groom was there, towering over everyone, laughing, holding out his hand, touching people as if to heal them. He shone with laughter and joy, and moved with the gentle, barely perceptible motions of large, shy men who rarely dance but are game to try when other people insist they do.

At last the bride appeared, cleaving past the woman with the expensive hat and her girlfriend who danced next to her in her show-girl heels. She came onto the floor like a train out of control, forcing gasps from the two women, and scattered applause from everyone else. Suddenly and ferociously, she began to dance.

Quintet

THE WOMAN WHO was not his wife owned a shop in Toronto where she sold overpriced glass objects and Brazilian amethysts to people who did not know what to do with their money. She was his mistress, but he never called her that; he called her Jill. Sometimes in the bedroom of her tiny condominium on the twenty-seventh floor above the harbour, he called her Kitten. His wife's name was Katherine, and sometimes he called his wife Kitten too. Katherine taught in the humanities department at the university and had recently defended a Ph.D. thesis on Theodor Adorno. His daughter's name was Jessica, and she was eighteen years old and lovely.

Raymond told himself that he did not put women in a hierarchy, he did not put beauty over intelligence, grace above modesty, or sex above stimulating conversation, but whenever he thought about the women in his life that is how they fell into place for him; Jill, in the downtown shop with new age music playing from speakers that couldn't be seen, selling Brazilian amethysts to people who didn't know what do with their money. Katherine with her ornate salads, a brilliant dressing

that people talked about, and the bottle of wine that took everyone by surprise. Jessica was simply Jessica. She was nearly
nineteen years old and she was lovely. Men stopped to look at
her; even women stopped to look at her.

Raymond stared at himself in the mirror, a Santa Claus
face covered in shaving cream. He scraped away swaths of it,
precisely, even surgically. He shaved the way a man prepares for
battle.

Katherine stood in the kitchen measuring out fifteen milli-
litres of Armagnac for her cassoulet — her "quick cassoulet,"
she called it, even though the recipe called for chorizo sausages,
goose fat, and cannellini beans that had been soaked for two
days. She had assembled the cassoulet the day before and
placed it in a gleaming stainless steel refrigerator. Dinner would
not be as special as it could have been. She had no desire to
intimidate the young man with a spectacular feast. Her husband
had his own reasons. Too much emphasis on this one meal in
particular, to "over-invest in it," would be a mistake. That is
what he said to her; "I don't think we should over-invest in
this one. Do you?" It was a warning to them.

Jessica had brought home young men before of course,
armies of them, too many to count, certainly too many to
remember their names. Katherine had fed them all, gladly,
and forgotten them. The appetites of young men pleased her.
They ate fast, even furiously, with smiles on their faces, uncer-
tain if they should ask for more, but always wanting more.
They did not pick at their food, they did not find fault with
it, they couldn't dream of finding fault with it. The army of
boys Jessica brought home, tall boys who stood nervously on
the carpet ... This one would be different; she and Raymond

understood that. He was twenty-one, an age that seemed ominous to them both, ancient even, and threatening. His name was Douglas. Not Doug. Jessica wanted this made clear. "It's Douglas," she said, emphatically. He rode a motorcycle; this had been the cause of the rift.

Raymond had not spoken in anger, but in the un-contradictable voice of a senior minister in government. "Absolutely not. I will not have my daughter skidding around on the back of a motorcycle driven by a twenty-one-year-old boy. I don't care if you're nearly nineteen," he told her. "When you are living in this house ... You know the rest of that argument already," he said. The discussion was over.

There had been a sulky fall out. A slammed door. The playing of loud music behind it. It was childish; it was hopeless. Jessica was in love. She had fallen, as if through ice, and was gone from her father into a place he couldn't follow. Katherine had more familiarity with this place. She had found it before several times, more times than she'd cared to let him know about. She had found it in the stacks at the Robarts library, in the arms of an older man, in Geneva she had found it, and in Vancouver. There was a time that she had found it in him, in the dark shadows of his face when they were both twenty-six years old and the cities of Europe were in his eyes, and on his cheekbones, the suffering of parents, of grandparents, and the cities on fire. He would rebuild those cities. That is what he told her, and that's what she saw in him.

She spoke to her husband on behalf of Jessica. She could not stop herself from recalling her own immense passage through British Columbia on the back of a Kawasaki. Up endless highways through places called Golden and Hope. The mountains flew up on all sides of her, and she was her daughter's age, slightly older. The boy's hair came out in shining curls beneath his helmet, the denim of her blue jeans gripped him. She could smell his body through the leather of his jacket. She could smell his sweat, and his hair. At night the stars hung like sponges for them as they lay in a sleeping bag. The mountain peaks were severe and white and in the morning they went naked together into the cold streams.

"You will lose her over this," she said, remembering.

RAYMOND FINISHED SHAVING and turned from the mirror. He did not like to look there anymore, as he once had. There was a degree of handsomeness required of a man, and he no longer achieved the top level of that. Still, there was something in the face that looked back at him that was undeniable. He imagined himself, three hours from now, when the dinner was done, driving along the lakeshore with the condominium project, *his* project, half-finished on the skyline, a light summer haze coming in off the water, the windows of the car up, and Dexter Gordon on the stereo, the remastered Blue Note recordings. Jill would be waiting for him, the wine open, she would be into her third glass, nursing it. Paul Simon on the stereo. He would not stay any longer than it took. She would see him off at the door wearing a pair of sweatpants, like a college girl, naked from the waist up, her breasts like the cupped fists of a child. She trained, she was extremely fit. Katherine had let that go and allowed herself liberties in that regard. Sometimes, at the worst of it, when they were both raging, he would shout at her that she was fat. Jill was not fat, not even close. She was constantly at the club. When they were through with each other she would hold the door open for him. "Behave yourself," she said strangely, whenever he left her apartment, as if he needed an excuse for having a wife and daughter. As if he needed sympathy for allowing that to happen to him. It annoyed him.

Raymond finished up in the bathroom, and changed his clothes. He would not over-do his clothes, and reminded himself that he was dressing not for Jessica's latest boyfriend, but for the woman who was not his wife. He heard music coming out from beneath his daughter's door, the jerkily sweet sound of the tenor saxophone, he could not make out who, Roland Kirk, maybe. Raymond could live with Roland Kirk, despite the excesses and the gimmicks. He knew his daughter was signalling her appreciation, and her acceptance of how it had worked out. It was not his music precisely, but it was close enough. Katherine had talked sense to him. She had always been a sensible woman. He admired that in her more than ever. He admired it the way he had once admired her shoulders.

THE DOORBELL RANG at six thirty and this did not go unnoticed.

"Punctual," said Katherine, swooping into the living room with a plate of brie she had warmed. She had not heard his motorbike either, and thought that was good manners, and good diplomacy on the boy's part, to come in quietly.

Raymond shouted up the stairs to his daughter. "Your friend is here." He chose his words carefully. It was a minefield: having daughters, when they grew up and became attractive.

Jessica loped downstairs wearing something skin-tight and shimmering on her legs, the sort of thing the woman who was not his wife would wear. It was the type of garment that meant sex, it could only mean sex, and he watched them come together in

the hall, the young man's black helmet knocking like a bowl-
ing ball against his knee. His daughter seemed to enter into
the surface of his body without touching him or even getting
particularly close to him.

Raymond shook the boy's hand and was startled by the
intensity of the grip, the sheer youth of it, like a cable that had
wrapped itself around his hand. He was forced to squeeze harder
in order not to be outdone.

"Raymond," he said.

"It's a pleasure, sir. In my opinion your project on the lake
is the only architecture in the city. Real architecture, I mean."

"Well," Raymond laughed. "Condos," he said, dismissively.
"For the very rich."

"Great condos," said the young man. "Rich or not, they're
places to live in. What's out there anymore is just engineering."

Raymond laughed again. "Let's not underestimate engineers." In fact he held engineers in total contempt.

"No, of course. You're right," the young man said.

"Is anyone hungry?" Katherine was not asking a question.
She was making a statement of truth.

"Starving," said the young man.

At the table things went well. Raymond felt an unaccountable
pride for his wife and his daughter, for their beauty and for
everything in the house. There was braided leather on the
wall, brought back from Montevideo, because they knew about
Uruguay and braided leather. His wife, in particular, knew
about the finer things. He felt pride in her. He felt pride even
in the woman who was not his wife, as if she were some crucial
support beam he'd had the foresight to install over the client's
objections.

Katherine felt herself to be smiling as well. Dinner was going brilliantly. The way it should. There was wine but it was nothing special, a white from Point Pelee, where they had gone years ago to see the birds when Jessica was young. The young man leaned into his food like an athlete, intense and blissful. He would not have wine, "not with the motorcycle," he said.

"Of course," Raymond answered quickly. Jessica had turned down the wine as well, and this annoyed Raymond briefly for reasons he could not put his finger on. It showed an over-allegiance that wasn't warranted, certainly not yet.

"This is incredible," cried the young man.

"Isn't it? My mom could have been secretary-general of the United Nations. Really. She gave it up to make the perfect cassoulet and to look after me and Daddy."

"Not perfect," said Katherine.

"Perfect. Beyond perfect," said the young man.

"She danced with Kofi Annan."

"Darling."

"She *did*. He made a pass at her."

Katherine laughed. She was shining now, like her daughter.

Raymond examined her with approval. Sometimes it surprised him to see that beauty had not yet washed its hands of his wife.

"It was a long time ago, and he didn't."

"He did."

Katherine laughed again. "He was a very good dancer," she said evasively.

There had been men who were not immune to her. Men who were the opposite of immune. A lieutenant general in the British foreign office had stood outside her door at the Biltmore wearing a cummerbund and holding a corkscrew and a twelve-hundred-dollar bottle of Petrus, begging to be let in, his accent barely comprehensible to her. There were ambassadors, and senior professors, there was a poet who was barely out of his teens and did not know how to drive. "You must leave your husband and marry me. I want you to marry me," he said. He had gone to his knees for her. She was four months pregnant with Jessica, and he did not have any socks. There had been men who wanted her with a desperation that she found difficult to believe. And then there was Jessica and a blurring of days into a soft and tedious thing that was her life, or at least the life that children gave you. She did not regret it. She gave up on French theory, she gave up on Walter Benjamin, and Julia Kristeva. There was Raymond, forever working and arcing his way into a senior partnership. And now there was this. Her life. She was fifty-eight years old and her doctorate was finally complete. Tenure was not around the corner. She wondered if Raymond was seeing someone but she did not wonder very much. She refused to have feelings about that.

DINNER ENDED WITH a crash of satisfaction that was audible. The young man attempted to help with the dishes, but Katherine shooed him away, almost sternly. Then Jessica and her friend were together, gathering themselves in front of the door. She was tying her hair back for the ride and he was watching her, intently. They seemed to press into each other like a form of matter that had been disunited.

"We'll be back before *you*, Dad." She laughed. "He works late on those condos. He always works late. He might as well be in the clubs."

Raymond, hovering, stepped forward to shake the young man's hand.

"Drive carefully," said Raymond. It was not a command. It was a statement of understanding between men. They shook hands again and this time Raymond was ready for it.

Katherine came forward, almost shyly, and lifted her hand. "It was pleasure to meet you, Douglas. I'm sure we'll see you again."

"You will. You definitely will," he said at once, thickly.

Raymond took his leave and bounded up the stairs. He picked up his briefcase, which was nearly empty. He'd made up his mind that he would not be condescended to by the woman who was not his wife. He would show her that there was nothing for him to be ashamed of; to be partnered in matrimony to a fine woman. There was nothing wrong with that. To have your child, beautiful and grown. It was she who had missed out, not him. How could he tell her that? The warm, unexpected presence of your child awakened by a dream, sliding beneath the covers next to you. Your wife's back rising and falling on the other side. Your daughter's miniature fingers tapping on your back, as if to make sure you were actually there. Her stuffed toy on your skin. How could he tell her that? Or anyone? There was nothing for him to be ashamed of. He stopped in the bathroom to take a look at his face. In the light from the hall he saw a tragic face. A man's face. He needed to think of a good reason for Katherine not to call him at the office.

KATHERINE STOOD IN the kitchen running water into the sink and staring out the window. It was getting dark so soon. She heard the scrabble of feet on loose stones and there was her daughter, entangled in the arms of her young man. With a sudden, almost military gesture, Jessica tugged on her helmet, her face disappeared under a gleaming black bulb. Katherine remembered such a gesture from before, the snap beneath the chin, and the thrill of it, like something made complete.

She watched as the young man mounted the motorcycle and Jessica followed, swinging her long leg over the saddle.

Raft

I'VE BEEN DOING this long enough to know a lot of people and a lot about what they get up to. I know the Sifton kid sells pot, and I've got an idea where he's growing it. I know Ruth Vankough- net's baby has an ear infection and the doctor expects it to clear up soon. I also know that on Friday night Honos Bruckner will start drinking and crying for his wife who left him fifty years ago, after the boys were killed. By Saturday there's a good chance he'll set the milk shed on fire. By Sunday afternoon his sister will be in from Ottawa to settle him down, and by Sunday night I'll be driving out there with the flashers on to make sure he doesn't blow his head off with the .32 Savage that he keeps wrapped up in burlap in the root cellar.

I also know that twice a week Mrs. Carruthers will call the station and lodge a complaint against teenagers. Mrs. Carruthers has a lot of complaints; it's a hobby for her. She complains about the playing of cards for money. She tolerates euchre at the seniors' centre on Saturday night, but playing cards for money is something that fills her with hate. She hates the government, the town, the two tennis courts the town put in by the lake;

she hates the lake and the fish that swim in it.

She lives alone in a bungalow by the beach, and twenty-five years ago her husband ran off with a tourist and moved into a trailer park in Pensacola, Florida. Normally that would be enough to fill a person up with hate, but people tell me that twenty-five years ago she hated him too, and cuffed him about the head with a length of board. Today what she hates most is teenagers, and twice a week she calls up the station, "This is Phyllis Carruthers and there's teenagers!" She makes it clear that being a teenager is already a violation of the law.

Connie takes the calls. Connie's the dispatcher and when things go crazy at the station she imitates the woman and says, "This is Phyllis Carruthers, and there's teenagers." What Mrs. Carruthers objects to about teenagers is that they drink. She suffers from glaucoma in both eyes but somehow she's still able to look out her front window and distinguish a beer can from ginger ale at a hundred paces. "They're drinkin', you get down here." It's because of her brother Raymond that she opposes drinking. Raymond got drunk at the Legion and ran into a bull moose on the road by the old roundhouse and now he's buried behind the baseball pitch with the Catholics.

Usually we don't do anything when Mrs. Carruthers calls, but sometimes we send a cruiser. The fact is teenagers *do* drink on the beach. They get drunk, they set a fire in a trash can, and then they run away. They don't do it a lot, but they do it. I did it when I was a teenager; me and my brother Jamie drank the old man's dandelion wine there and got so drunk that Jamie prayed out loud to God that if He stopped him from being sick, he'd never get drunk again. That was thirty years ago and today Jamie's sitting in the tavern with a wad of

lottery tickets in front of him, trying to bum cigarettes off
people.

I was thinking about this when Connie came on the radio.

"We have Phyllis Carruthers," she announced flatly. "And
there's *teenagers*." By then I was on my way to the next county to
see about Willy Costello's dog bite. It was Willy's firm belief that
if you got bit by a dog, you gained the uncontested legal right to
shoot up its owner's house with a rifle.

The day was stifling and marsh hawks flew a half a mile in the
air, circling on the thermals. I took the Carruthers call, turned
the cruiser around in the parking lot of the church, and drove
back to the beach outside of town.

YEARS AGO THE sawmill sat on that beach. When it closed the
shore was left a mess of sawdust, board ends, horseshoes, and
old whisky bottles filling up with sand. After a while the trees
grew back and the town put up a sign saying it was a park now.
I learned to swim in that park, caught my first sunfish in the
reeds. We undressed in the beach house with the concrete
floor. Two peepholes were gouged in the girls' side at about
the height of a fourteen-year-old boy, and a spiderweb hung
from a corner with a spider folded up in the middle of it,
waiting. It was dark and sour with old pee, so you changed fast
and ran out of there with your feet slapping on the cold concrete.
No matter what, you always lost a sock.

Driving there made all that come back. I saw the raft, like
a tabletop, fifty feet off shore, looking exactly like the raft that
was chained there when I was a kid. Every night it got splat-
tered with gull shit, and every morning the lifeguard washed it
off. Now there was a patch of Astroturf nailed on top, and it was

packed with kids; some stood, some flipped over backwards, others jumped up and down and screamed. The Bennett girl was out there and she had on a bathing suit like the kind she shouldn't have, and Jeff Huddy's kid leaned on her in a way that he shouldn't have. A dog allowed itself to be spun like a Frisbee from the raft and hurled into the water. The rest of the kids were squared off like gangsters, holding whispered life-and-death conversations.

It was just an old raft for playing on but it was also a launching pad for every scheme a kid ever gets up to: boys were out there plotting to shake their virginity, girls exchanged silver, magical words. I could see already the Bennett girl would not finish school, she'd serve coffee at Steadman's while her mother looked after the baby. The Huddy boy would drive a pickup he had not paid for and tell people he was going to get a job at the Tembec plant in Temiscaming. The O'Malley twins sat shoulder to shoulder, conspiring to smoke a cigarette behind the old train station, which has been turned into a boutique now and is where the kids go when they want to get up to something.

FOR TEN MINUTES I watched them swooping in and out like huge gulls, waiting for the raft to empty so they could take their turn; and it wasn't just the kids I was watching, it was their futures too. I sat in the cruiser with the air conditioner on, and then reached beside me for the bulletproof jacket. It's regulation that we wear them now. I put on the vest, opened the car door, and nearly stepped on the woman.

She lay on a beach towel on the grass, well-tanned, dark-haired, wearing a red, two-piece bathing suit with flowers painted on it. She was reading a novel about vampires. I didn't know what to say, so I gave her a stiff nod and muttered, "Hi, there ..."

She flopped the book down in front of her. "Hi there," she said. "It's hot, huh?" The sweat must have been already leaking from my vest.

"Yeah, it's hot. It's always hot this time of year." That sounded like a stupid thing to say to a woman sunbathing in late July. "Around *here*," I added.

"Oh, I love it. I just love the heat." She smiled.

She'd been smiling since I got out of the car. That was something I noticed, along with the fact that she was not wearing a ring, and that her teeth were white and big, and that when she smiled it was hard to think about anything else.

Across the beach a young mother dipped her daughter feet-first into the water and gleefully yanked her away. Behind her two boys, like bronco riders, whiplashed themselves on yellow ducks mounted on springs. The beach gave way to the pines, then the hill by the seniors' home, then the church. The air over the tin roof rippled in the heat.

When I turned, the woman was still smiling and looking as though she expected me to say something.

"We got a call about some kids drinking on the beach."

She nodded and peered over her shoulder as if she might be able to spot one for me. Maybe it was the heat, or her bathing suit, or the bulletproof jacket, but I didn't want to move. I wanted to stand there and talk to her.

"I had a few drinks myself on this beach when I was a kid, so I wouldn't want to come down too hard on anyone."

"Oh, sure, I know what you mean." She shifted on the towel

as if she expected me to lie down next to her. "It's not the end of the world, is it?"

"You're right, it's not. It's just, you know, we've got these old-timers who live along here. They don't like it too much."

I indicated back to the houses along the road. Pete Rickey was out there, folded into a ratty sofa he kept on the lawn. The rains had swollen it like a sponge, and he sat there hunched in his overalls with a bottle between the cushions. Rickey was an old, bad wino and every day in the summer he sat in that sofa, sneaking drinks and eyeballing the girls on the beach.

"If you ask me, it's some of these old-timers you've got to look out for. Not the kids." The woman inched forward on the towel and nodded behind me to the Rickey place. "That old man there, on that couch? He came over, he was standing right where you are. He stood there five minutes looking down the front of my bathing suit. I swear, that's what he was doing."

"Yeah, well, you've got to be careful with some of these guys."

"Oh, I'm not worried about him. He's just an old drunk. I can take care of him. It gives me the creeps, though."

I imagined it would give you the creeps. Pete Rickey was a creepy old guy with a dark cloud that festered around his head like a swarm of hornets. I didn't know what to say next. I wanted to say something easy and sincere. But all that came out of my mouth was a sigh, as though the vest was forcing the air out of me. "I better get up the beach and check things out."

"Sure. Well, good luck." She kept on with the enormous smile, then reached for the vampire book and pulled it to her.

THE BEACH WAS crammed with kids getting ready to go home. First I nodded at the Murphy boy, then waved to Mrs. Dombrosky, who sat in her car with the air conditioner on while she kept an eye on the grandkids. I told the Gigantes girl to stay out of trouble. "Oh yeah, right," she shot back, and sat down at a picnic table with her girlfriends. I nodded to Sean Gregory Philips, who broke into Steadman's for a carton of cigarettes last year, and was supposedly training for the reserves at Petawawa.

No one on that beach was drinking anything stronger than a Slurpee or bottled spring water, and I didn't care if they were. What I cared about was the woman back there on the beach towel. I cared about what to say to her. "Are you from around here?" How about, "Oh, you're reading a book about vampires." I could've told her what I heard from the highway guys after they dug up the pioneer cemetery and found stakes driven through the ribs of the old skeletons. They did that to keep their souls from the vampires — that's what they said. The pioneers around here had a belief in that sort of thing. I could have told her that.

The beach ended by Herman Lepitskie's broken old scow and at that point I turned around. There wasn't anybody doing anything along there except yelling, swimming, planning their first misdemeanours, and getting sunburns. It was just Phyllis Carruthers again, phoning up the station so that she could have someone to complain to, or just someone to talk to. I passed the old beach house on the way back and my mind was made up; I'd go back there to the cruiser and I'd ask that woman in the red bathing suit out. I saw myself as she would in size eleven black shoes, with my body armour on, and a Sigarms duty pistol strapped to my hip. I'd ask her out anyway.

Out by the tennis courts a late-model Ford made a turn

around the water treatment plant. She was her driving it, with her hair curling around her face. She saw me and waved out the window, and then she was gone.

For a moment a breeze came off the lake but it didn't cool a thing. All it did was move the heat around me.

I GOT BACK in the cruiser and sat there. Almost at once I saw a woman coming at me from between the trees. She was bent, and old, and moving hard along the foot path from the end of the beach, and she was wearing what looked like a hospital gown. When she got closer I saw it wasn't a hospital gown she had on, but an old dress, and that the woman was Esther Bruckner who lives at the seniors' place now, and used to be married to old Honos. She was flushed red at the neck and looked desperate to say something.

What I know about Esther Bruckner is the same as what I know about Honos — that many years ago her two boys died in a house fire. People around here say they "got burnt ... those two boys what got burnt." For some reason they never say, "those two boys who died in a house fire." When it happened they were living in a shack by the O'Grady settlement and Esther had to walk a half mile for well water each morning. It was while she was doing that the shack caught fire, a pine shack, with the pine resins going up like gasoline. No one could get near the place until after sundown, when the heat finally cooled, and that's when the men went in and found them; the two boys under a blackened table, sitting together on the floor.

I got out from the cruiser and stood in front of her but she had already stopped. She seemed to have no intention of going any farther than me.

"The Virgin Mary," she gasped. "The Virgin Mary was stood on a tree and that tree bent down to where them flames was, you understand? Wherever it was the Blessed Virgin went, that tree went too. No further than what she did. Right to the flames." She trembled enormously. Her face was creased and her eyes showed small and bright as a weasel's. "It was the same day as the apparitions, you know, the day it happened ... when the flames come to where the Virgin was, and the little children was called for. Tommy and Joe ... You saw them rings around the sun. The day the apparitions come! It was that day ... you understand?" She aimed a spotted brown hand at the sky and nodded so sharply that I nodded back.

"Yes, ma'am," I said. "I understand." She seemed satisfied by this, because she turned from me and shrank away.

I saw the raft pitching on the water, and it seemed to me that maybe I did understand — at least something of what a person goes through, and the heat in summer, and why Honos was a lonely drunk with a rifle and a case of beer in the root cellar, and a two-hundred-acre farm that had gone to bush a long time ago. I saw Esther between the pines by the seniors' place, a young woman, with her hands at her face. Her home was a flaming heap of timbers, and from inside it she heard the cries of her boys pitch across the sky. Tommy and Joe were in there, they would always be in there, hiding on the floor beneath the table, in each other's arms.

The Haw Eaters

MY NAME IS Stephanie Houghton and to my knowledge I am
one of several illegitimate great-granddaughters of the Duke
of Northumberland, the first Duke of Northumberland, the
one convicted of treason and hanged. My mother has always
insisted on this, although my father, for some reason, maintains
that I am actually the bastard child of a South African prostitute. This bit of knowledge is something I have not passed on to
my daughter, who is now sitting at my feet while I write this. My
father, for better or worse, is still alive, a retired mechanical
engineer born in Germany. He courted my mother in Durban,
South Africa and moved to Canada, to a farm outside Toronto
where I was born.

When I was a child, my three sisters, me, and my brother
who is dead now, did our homework grouped beneath one light
bulb, to save on electrical expenses. To my father electricity
was more precious than blood or gold and he often circled
about the table where we worked, and randomly boxed us on
the ear. When his temper got the better of him, which happened
frequently, or when his children defied him in any way, which

also happened frequently, he climbed up on the back of a winged armchair and roared like a beast.

Despite this, I have maintained a relationship with the old man, who still lives in the same farmhouse on the same forty acres outside of the city. In 1954, in what I sometimes think was an act of personal retribution against my father, Hurricane Hazel swept through a corridor of southern Ontario and took down every tree on his property, leaving it appraised at ten per cent of what he paid for it. This, of course, did nothing to soften his ways. Today, despite being a feeble old man, he remains as unrepentant, unpredictable, and ferocious as ever. When I get angry with him, which is often, I leave the house as a pre-caution, to make sure I don't murder the man. Two Thanksgivings ago, in a state of fury, I chased him into the backyard with a ball-peen hammer, but in the end I managed to contain myself and no harm was done.

WHEN I WAS thirteen years old my brother died of late childhood leukemia, and after that my mother retired to the basement and began to consume large amounts of red wine. She did this secretly, with the connivance of me and my sisters who helped her hide the empty bottles from our father, and arranged to buy new ones for her with the aid of our friends' older brothers and sisters. My mother never recovered from Michael's death, and at some point began to grind prescription pharmaceuticals into a solution and inject them into her arm. There were times that I found her in the basement, clutching her knees, weeping or singing, with her kit and a drop of blood on the floor beside her.

For years we secretly and not so secretly prayed for our father to drop dead. These days we feel no obligation to keep

this information from him. "Dad," we remind him, cheerfully, "we used to pray that you would die." My father takes
this news with a tilt of his head, and smiles as though being
complimented on his skills as a parent. In the end it was not
him, but my mother who died: she died suddenly from a brain
tumour at the age of thirty-eight. All her life my mother had
been fascinated by the human brain, and then the doctors
discovered a brain tumour the size of a hazelnut. Eleven days
later she was dead.

AFTER MY MOTHER died there was nothing left for me in that
house and on the stroke of my eighteenth birthday I left home
and moved to a bungalow on Ward's Island in Lake Ontario
off the shores of Toronto. I was then a towering, bright-faced,
enthusiastic virgin. I mingled ardently with anarchists, pot
smokers, environmentalists, followers of Wilhelm Reich,
vegans, and disaffected *Globe and Mail* reporters. Immediately
I fell in love with a forty-year-old poet who was fond of saying
poetical things to me. For example, he called me his "little
untilled garden."

By that point my virginity had taken on almost feudal dimen-
sions, and I was determined to shed myself of it once and for
all. My plan was simple; I would follow my poet by train to
Kingston, where he had gone to teach European literature
to summer students. There, in the romance of that distant city
made of limestone, I would bed the man I loved.

Before I could put this plan into action, I met a man who
was not a poet, but a sailor, who owned his own boat moored
in a slip at the Island Marina, and wore a red kerchief around
his throat and played an antique tenor guitar. He also happened

to be sailing to Kingston the following week, so it turned out I would not have to buy a train ticket after all.

With the wind whipping at my hair and the blue reaches of Lake Ontario glinting in all directions, my virginity did not withstand the three-day sail to Kingston. I enthusiastically surrendered it while moored off a heron rookery on the shoreline of Prince Edward County. The rocks were stained with guano and the shrieking of those hungry birds combined with the raucous cries of my own lovemaking made a sound that was unforgettable to me. When it was over I told my sailor friend that it felt like I had just been scratched in the exact spot where I had always itched. He laughed.

The following afternoon I landed at Kingston harbour, beneath the looming thick walls of the federal penitentiary. Flushed with excitement, matured by my recent experience, and immensely impressed with myself, I leapt on a bus to Queen's University and found my poet in the middle of his second-year lecture on Christian morality in the `novels of Dostoevsky. I paced in the hall until he was finished.

"Guess what?" I blurted, almost before he'd made it through the door.

It seems to me now that my virginity had posed an ethical problem to the man. Some remnant of gallantry, embarrassment, confusion, and plain egg-headedness had stalled him on the path to becoming my first lover. In *my* eyes the fault lay with my bothersome virginity, and now that I had done away with it, I was eager to put into motion what I trusted would be a succession of vigorous affairs with poets, scholars, sailors, eco-terrorists, and other men who were tall.

To my surprise, my poet-boyfriend was unimpressed with

my new status and I sensed a chill coming off him. Chill or not, I went immediately back to his rooms and made love to him. When it was over, gripped by curiosity, I could not resist asking,

"How was it for you?"

My poet was appalled by this question and gave me a narrow, horsy look and reached for his Dostoevsky. "You've got a long way to go," he said.

Coming home together on the train he was sullen, unapproachable, and more interested in Dostoevsky's *The Possessed* than in anything I had to say to him. "A single page of Dostoevsky would crush all of them." From Kingston to Toronto those were the only words he spoke to me. At Union Station, after whispering something I couldn't make out, he slipped into the subway. I never saw him again.

The week's experience had left me with an ectopic pregnancy. Five days later, delirious, in a fever, and dressed in a T-shirt and blue jeans, I boarded an island ferry on a windy day, determined to take myself to the nearest hospital. Onboard, an elderly woman appraised me in a way that was concerned and contemptuous at the same time.

"You young people today, you just don't *care* about the cold, do you?" It turned out that I had a fever of a hundred and four. I fainted in the waiting room of St. Michael's Hospital.

THESE DAYS I am a married woman (not exactly married) and live on Manitoulin Island in a solar-powered house that smells of wood smoke, herbal tea, and beeswax. On two occasions my husband has brought down a deer with a crossbow from our bedroom window. He dresses them himself. His name is

Martin; he's an environmentalist and self-described "Polack lawyer." Actually he's a Kaszub; his ancestors fled the Kaszubi mountain region a century and a half ago and settled in eastern Ontario at Wilno. "I'm the only Polack lawyer on the island," he states proudly. "Just ask for the Polack lawyer. They'll know who you mean." He is the father of my daughter and we have been together for eight years now, although the prospect of sleeping each night with the same man still alarms me. I'm the sort of woman who needs to graze, and I have warned him about this repeatedly.

My daughter is six and possesses the Island moniker of *Muukwa*, which, I understand, means "bear" in the Algonkian language. We chose the name after a bear reared up and placed its paws on the back door of the house at the exact moment I went into labour. Its claws popped through the screen one at a time, and probably it would have entered the room had not the midwife and Martin hurled a stack of shoes and boots at it.

Recently Martin and I had a ghastly fight about an animal seen out that same door. Martin insisted it was a Dexter cow belonging to a neighbour. I insisted it was a bear. I also insisted that after eight years as an honorary Haw Eater, which is the name that native-born islanders give to themselves, I might know the difference between a bear and a Dexter cow. Things got nasty and I made several wild remarks. Finally, two cups of steaming tea were made and carried to the sofa and an appeasement took place there. We are still together.

THESE DAYS MY daughter is crowned by an astonishing head of yellow curls. She sits beside me on the floor bringing to life a series of inanimate objects, and conducting short and formal discussions with each of them.

"Good morning, Mr. Pee. Are we feeling good today? Mr. Pee has to poo," she announces gravely. She is a genuine Haw Eater, conceived and born on Manitoulin Island, and raised on haw berry jam. She is the sort of child who stops complete strangers on the street, grabs their hands and yells, "I'm shy, I'm shy!" All morning she sits on the floor playing peacefully. Then, out of the blue she jumps to her feet and shouts,

"You're not going to die, Mommy, right?"

I lean down and scratch her head. "No, baby, not me. I'll never die. I'll always be here to love you up."

She smiles fiercely at me. "Yeah," she says, "yeah!"

She pulls herself away from me and prepares to fling herself from the back of a chair. To assist with this she has tied a dish-towel around her neck and made a superhero's cape of it.

"Into *in-fin-it-y!*" she shouts, and hurls her little body at the air.

Whistling Down the Lights

ON A TRAIN eastbound at Minaki, Ontario I knock into a man who wears a squared, black hat that is not so much a cowboy hat as an Indian hat. He is drunk or close to it, having sat for two hundred miles in the club car with a young, shifty-looking man who claims to be Yugoslavian, and buys him one drink after another. By the time I bump into him, the man in the square black hat sways in the aisle, as does everybody else on this train. All of us are as drunk as bush pilots, or at least we appear to be as the thin train clatters over the Canadian Shield.

Without being asked he explains to me that he is on his way to visit his sister who lives in Kingston. "Where the jail is, the Big House," he clarifies and laughs coldly, followed by a smoker's hack. It's not clear whether this sister is a blood sister or some other kind of sister; or whether she will be there at the station waiting for him or, for that matter, whether she herself is an inmate of the Kingston jail. It turns out he didn't let her know he was coming. Or he did let her know, at least he tried by mail or telephone, this is not clear either, but was unsuccessful. Also, he has no idea where she lives, and of course this is his first visit to the city, to any city.

Things like this happen all the time and I feel sorry for the man. I'm left with a sense of things evaporating into time, things that are no longer what they were, like the young man from a few hours earlier who insisted fiercely that he was a Yugoslavian, not a Bosnian, not a Croat or Serb, but a Yugoslavian, even though his country has been taken over by men who blow up libraries and shoot people in cold blood. These two men share a common loss of country, and maybe I share it too. Maybe everyone on this train shares it and that's why I'm sitting here shoulder to shoulder with a stranger; because he is part of me, just as we are part of that dark-eyed man who is now roaring drunk wearing a T-shirt with *Megadeth* printed on it and defiantly singing Yugoslavian folk songs from the club car on a train, forty kilometres north of Pickle River, Ontario.

FOR SOME REASON we get talking about the northern lights; in particular the sound of the northern lights. I tell him they sound like the rustling of a dress, though truthfully I've never heard them. In 1999, while camped at the Shoals near Chapleau, Ontario, I watched the night sky turn into a prancing red horse that shed enough light to read a book by. A young German woman from Leipzig crawled out of her tent, stood straight as a pole, staring up at the universe, and began to cry. But I had never heard the northern lights before. It's an affectation of mine, especially after a few drinks, to try and appear close to the land or at least knowledgeable about matters of the bush and the universe.

The man in the black square hat pays no attention to me. He's not the slightest bit interested in whether I'm close to the land or not. He's not even listening; in fact he interrupts me.

"If you want to see the northern lights, eh, what you do is whistle. You just whistle." He says this to me as though offering a piece of canonical wisdom that has been passed down to him through the generations. But there's something mocking in his voice, as if he knows this wisdom is corrupted now and exists only because of a white man's need to hear such things. There is something sad and hopeless about this state of affairs, but I can't put my finger on it and neither can he.

I also knew that one day I'll try it. One day when I feel that everything is entirely foreign, and I'm just a man killing time in the Quebec Airport, with a crushed ketchup package on the plate in front of me, and two Jazz pilots getting drunk at the next table, I will whistle the same self-conscious notes a person whistles on a Toronto streetcar to make himself come true, or at least to remind himself he's still there. I'll invite the world to jump into my lap like a puppy. Nothing will happen. The sky will remain vaulted, the conductor in a monotone will say, "Sudbury, Sudbury Avenue next stop," and I'll tell myself this whistling down the lights is a Native matter, like dropping bone ashes or tobacco into the teeming rapids at Lachine to calm them. It won't work for me because I'm not a participant in that dialogue. Maybe it worked for Radisson or Brûlé, or some other white guy who had his fingers hacked off by the Iroquois, but it won't work for me.

THE DARK BECOMES a tent pitched over top of us; a small group of men engaged in the exchange of stories that involve the bush, animals, and weapons, and usually begin like this: "Me and my brother-in-law, right? We're fishing specs and he's got a .300 Savage propped up against a tree." Someone lights a cigarette in the darkness of the dome car, which is not something that is supposed to be done. The lighter flares against the walls and briefly reveals a group of men crouched in a prehistoric cave, waving their hands excitedly as they fix the ochre forms of great animals against rock walls by torchlight. And that's what we're doing. A hundred thousand years later beneath the flare of a disposable lighter, we're still at it. "Me and my brother-in-law, we're on a timber road outside Foleyet, I got a .303 Remington in the trunk —"

The man in the square black hat takes his turn and talks about moose hunting outside a reserve near Wapekeka. A fisherman from Brampton interrupts him right away, wants to know what sort of rifle he was using. The man is perplexed by the question and the story falters. He isn't sure what kind of rifle it was. That's not the point: only a white man would want to know what kind of rifle it was. He can't remember. Maybe it was a Mossberg thirty-thirty, or maybe it was a three hundred Savage. What's the difference?

A retired bus driver from Rivers, Saskatchewan gets in on it next. His voice is level and rhythmic as though driving buses most of his life across prairie flatland has smoothed all the high notes out of it. People listen to a man like this. "I don't hunt no more," he says slowly, "but I used to, back when. I'd get myself a deer. You forget how strong an animal your deer is." There's a general nod of agreement to this statement, even by me, though I've never held a rifle in my life. "I got him lined up, I got a bead on him, I fire, he just folds up, completely folds up. I aimed, fired, completely folded that deer up. He's spinning through the air, the dust flying. He stops spinning, hits the ground completely folded up. I run over. I got my knife out, I'm ready to slit his throat. What's he do? He shakes his head, gets up on his feet and goes running off. I'm telling you this deer was folded up. Now it's running off. Me, I got my rifle leaning against the half ton where I left it."

Another story is told by a truck driver about his run from Yorkton to Hudson Bay. He encounters a moose up front in the headlights and brakes to a stop. It's rutting season and the animal charges. The trucker cranks the horn, flashes his lights, but the moose closes. At ten metres the trucker jumps from the cab: the moose strikes the front and rides up the canopy. But somehow the glass holds and the massive animal collapses dead on the highway. "I try not to drive at night anymore," he says.

SOON THE OBSERVATION car is nearly empty. Someone unseen talks sporadically in the dark. I haven't the faintest idea where we are anymore. On the Shield, of course. Perhaps near a whistle stop at Nakina or beyond it. But what is Nakina? A hunter's shack? A word in Cree or Ojibway or Oji-Cree, or Scottish? Slowly, methodically, the man in the black hat stands up and scours the black, fast-moving outdoors. He stares deeply into it, eager to say something. At last he speaks; his lips tremble, like fingers tracing over a keyboard, searching for the perfect note. "This is beautiful land. I know this land, we used to come here. It's ..."

He tries to say something more, he tries to say out loud what it means to him; this club moss, the black ridge of boreal trees, the three-billion-year-old rocks and the water that is pitch black and seems to exist only so that people can drown in it. He wants to let everyone know this, to touch what's going on outside the window with language and with his fingers and give shape to it, but he can't. It's not the words that defeat him, but the country, the land itself.

He looks at it racing backwards through the window and sees the shadows brush against the train like a great, crouching animal made of obsidian. The trunks of the black spruce are fire-blasted, the granite gorges itself from the moss. Even the blue skin and the spongy, white flesh of pickerel are visible to him. He was an infant in a diaper, staring with immense eyes at the severed heads of fish; the pink and blue slush of their innards heaped on an old newspaper going dark with the slime. His mother laughed at his astonishment. He wants all of that to come together for him. "This is beautiful land," he tries again.

But that's not it either. It's not a question of beauty. It's got nothing to do with that. It has something to do with the treeline which is black and jagged, the empty fifty-gallon oil drums, and portable trailers that are not portable anymore, hydro trans-formers that march like giant skeletons over the land, black tar, bales of car tires, broken kitchen tiles, empty paint cans and the clattering of grasshoppers, abandoned air compressors in a field of burnt sage ...

He reaches out in front of him to grab this with his two hands, curling and uncurling his fingers. "I know this land," he pleads. "We used to ... we used to come here ..."

I'm Not Very Good at It

MY WIFE DRAGS me out to the Tenth Annual Safe-Sex fundraiser and she's got me in there shaking hands like I'm a politician.

"This is Lola," she says.

I shake hands with Lola. Lola's eighty-four years old and runs a brothel near the airport.

"When I was twenty-six," says Lola. "I was in New York, walking on the street, Fifth Avenue it was, and a young painter wanted to paint me. That was sixty-two years ago, and he just wanted to paint me. In oils."

My wife tells me that Lola's doing business again, at eighty-four.

"We're so proud of you, Lola. And you look great. Doesn't she look great?"

I say sure. She looks great. She doesn't look a day over eighty-four.

"I like Indians from India," says Lola. "They know how to treat an old woman best."

THEN I'M SHAKING hands with Black Horse Dancing.

"This is Black Horse Dancing," says my wife.

"Hi," I say. "I'm Jack."

Black Horse Dancing is a white guy with a shaved head. He's wearing a tight red miniskirt like the kind I wish my wife would wear, but she won't anymore.

"You look marvellous in that skirt," my wife says. "And you're not wearing makeup either. I like that."

"Oh, I don't need no makeup, baby." Black Horse Dancing starts to jerk up and down like he's dancing. And I guess that's what he's doing. He's one of those people you read about in magazines, who can't live unless they're dancing. He's also a junkie; gets his methadone dispensed from a paper cup twice a week at the clinic. What do I care? I just stand back so he doesn't poke my eye out with his dancing.

My wife whispers to me, "Black Horse Dancing is one of the great dancers in the city. He's a legend."

"I thought you said he was a junkie?" I whisper back.

"What's your point?" she says.

THEN I GET introduced to Tiffany. Tiffany's a prostitute, but I'm not supposed to call her that. "Call her a whore, a ho, a pro, or a hooker," my wife tells me. "But really you should call her a sex-trade worker, because that's what she is."

"I just got my tits done," says Tiffany.

My wife says, "Tiffany, this is Lola."

"Hello," says Lola. "When I was twenty-six I was in New York, walking on Fifth Avenue I believe, and a young painter wanted to paint me. That was sixty-two years ago, and he just wanted to paint me. In oils."

AFTER A COUPLE of minutes my wife, Tiffany, Lola, and a few other people and I sit down at a table at the front, talking and drinking soda water out of paper cups. From there I get a good gander at the situation. What I'm looking at here is a room full of sex-trade workers. I can tell they're sex-trade workers because they've all got cellphones attached to their bodies. They're ringing like crazy. One woman's deep in talk. Her phone starts ringing and she scoops it, gunslinger style, out of a holster strapped to her thigh.

"Yes? Yes … This is Roxy. Yes. Thursday? Thursday nine o'clock? Oh, that's good. Oh, that's very good," she croons and puts the phone back in the holster. That sort of thing's going on all around. About every kind of sex-trade worker there is is hanging out there. There's your extremely fat female sex-trade worker with fishnet stockings and a tattoo on her cleavage. Her name's Velvita and she's your basic "crack-ho," my wife explains, but she's been off it for a while, and all the girls are pulling for her. Then there's your bondage people, and video stars, and skinny sex-trade workers, and junkie ones, standing together in a separate corner of the room. Then there's your boys. About a half-dozen of them squeezed on a sofa, yakking away and answering cellphones.

"Don't the boys look marvellous tonight," my wife says. She calls them "the boys." Sure, I say, they look fine. What do I care? They're all wearing black shoes, black jeans, white T-shirts, sunglasses, telephones, and black leather jackets that say *University of Toronto* on the back.

"Fifth Avenue, I believe it was," says Lola to no one in particular. "I was twenty-six years old at the time and he just wanted to paint my picture. In oils."

I take a bite out of my paper cup and start chewing on it. My wife and Tiffany are talking about Tiffany getting her tits done. I'm looking around and I see someone I've seen before, leaning against the wall by the door. Good looking woman. A pound, maybe a pound and a half overweight, but who cares? Straight dark hair. And eyes. I mean *eyes*. She's using them to look at me. First she looks at me. Then she looks at my wife. Then she looks somewhere else. My wife's stopped talking for a bit, so I nudge her.

"Who's that?"

"Who?"

"By the door. The young one. I met her. I met her at the Christmas party."

"Oh. Her. I told you. Her name's Colleen. She's a meth freak."

"Right, Colleen."

My wife puts her hand under the table and touches my thigh.

"You hit on that skanky little bitch and I'll change the locks again."

She would, too. I know her.

"Fine," I say, "only how come she's a meth freak and that makes her a skanky bitch? And that other guy, he's a junkie, and he ends up being a legend?"

"Don't start, okay?"

Fine. I won't start.

"Why don't you circulate? Meet some people. You're not very good at that."

I GET UP and start to circulate. I circulate right on over to Colleen.

"Hi, I'm Jack."

"I know, I remember you."

"Yes, I remember you too. From the Christmas party."

We don't say anything. I'm looking at her. She's looking at me. It's mutual.

I'm looking at her eyes. There's a depth to them. I'm thinking it might be nice to plumb those depths.

"You survived the winter all right?" I try.

"Yes. The winter treated me all right. When I *let* it."

I like that. *When I let it*. Speaks volumes. "I know what you mean." We don't say anything after that and it's a bit awkward. I'm trying to think what to say to her.

"I should go help out in the kitchen. I'm glad I saw you again, Jack."

I'm glad too. I tell her that. She goes into the kitchen, and I'm standing there by myself.

Circulate, I think.

I circulate out the front door and have a smoke.

I'M OUT THERE standing on Church Street having a smoke. There's a dozen other people out there with cellphones attached to them. Also having smokes. They're all talking. Some are talking on the phone. Some are talking to each other. A tall woman is talking, shouting really.

"The guy says he wants to bring the dog around, right? Just wants to bring his dog around. That's what he says to me. I say forget it. You know me and animal rights. I mean, I totally live for that, right? Look, Mac, I say, I mean, I got to tell him. So I say, forget it. I'm totally into animal rights, just forget it. Don't even think about it. So pow. Gone. Two hundred bucks. Asshole," she says.

I toss the butt to the curb and go back inside.

ONCE I GET in I hang around for a minute in the lobby in front of the Community Billboard, reading the notices tacked on it. There's a notice for a seminar on the Hepatitis B vaccine. There's a poetry workshop for Lesbians of Colour. A seminar on "How to Stamp out Lesbophobia." A workshop on the herpes virus. A musical art therapy session for incest survivors. There's something called "Bashing the Bashers." There's a healing circle for people who are HIV positive, and a Native Canadian Sunrise and Sweetgrass Smudging ceremony. A Take-Back-the-Night plenary session. There's a support group for Single Mothers Against Deadbeat Dads (SMADD). A support group for Transgendered Ojibway. There are support groups for people who've been victimized by random violence, cyclical violence, family violence, systemic violence, endemic violence, media violence, emotional violence, and non-physical violence. There's even a call for submissions to a journal. "All submissions must be female appropriate," it says.

What do I know?

I GET BACK into the room and Tiffany and my wife are talking about men. Tiffany says pets are better. My wife's not sure. Lola's talking to someone I don't know. She tells him how she was walking on a street in New York, sixty-two years ago.

Where's the food, I'm thinking. Right then, the food comes in. It gets wheeled into the corner by the caterer, a bald guy wearing a suit jacket with big fins on the collar. He looks like a gangster. He probably *is* a gangster. I don't care what he is. I'm starving.

We all get up and take a plate and stand in line in the corner.

"Don't worry, folks, anything left over I take down to St. Francis Table," says the caterer. He's taking the lids off things: chicken, pasta, salad ...

I get back to the table and Tiffany's already there. She's got the biggest plate of food I've ever seen. It's stacked a foot high.

"You must be hungry."

"Not really. I'm a binge eater. What I do is starve myself until I have these like religious visions and then after that I binge. I don't *do* moderation," she explains, and burrows into the food. I'm packing into it pretty good too. People are talking.

"We were on a train going to Spokane, Washington, playing bridge," says Lola.

Tiffany says she's had the cramps for a week.

Someone tells her to take a Tylenol.

Someone else suggests Advil.

"Then I got involved with a Scotch and Soda Englishman, Regina, 1934. Gave me a genuine Hudson's Bay seal coat with a fox collar." Things go on like that for about twenty minutes. The food's done. I'm getting bored. My wife is too.

"Well," she says. "I think it's time to go." We get up together and start going around the room saying goodbye to people. She hugs and kisses them. I shake their hands.

OUTSIDE IT'S COLD, and snow's starting to slant down from the buildings. We walk a block to the car. My wife turns the engine over and lets it idle for a while, and then we're heading home on Wellesley Street. Out the window I see a guy lying on the sidewalk clutching his knee. His bicycle is wrapped around a traffic light, and the guy who did it is out of his car, standing with his arms folded, looking off into nowhere. In a second floor window I see a little girl with her arm stuffed elbow deep into a bag of potato chips.

"Lola's right. She's absolutely right." My wife's got this tone to her voice and she's staring very hard into the windshield.

"Right about what?"

"About India. About Indian men knowing how to treat older women. Not like here. Here, men have no idea."

I'm from here, so I take this a bit personally.

"Wait a minute. You know what they do to women in India? I'll tell you what. They set them on fire. They put them on a boat full of twigs, set them on fire and push them down a river. The River Ganges or something. I read about it. They've even got a word for it, it's called *kootay*, or *pootay* or something like that."

My wife is not impressed.

"The word is *sati*," she says coolly. "It was legally abolished over a century ago."

There's a heavy, uncomfortable feeling in the car now, so I look out the window and keep my mouth shut. I mean, what do I really know about setting women on fire?

WE GET HOME without saying a word. I don't want to but I'm thinking about a long time ago, when I first met her and couldn't take my eyes off her.

My wife goes into the bathroom and brushes her teeth. When she's finished I go in and brush mine, too. Then I go into her bedroom. She's already got her clothes off and is lying on her side under a cotton sheet. She's in a mood.

I lie down beside her with my clothes still on. Her breath is heavy coming out from somewhere in her throat.

"I'm going to end up just like her," she whispers.

"Like who?" I try.

"I'm going to end up just like Lola. I'm going to be old. I'm going to be ugly. People are going to laugh at me. I'm going to be just like her. Alone. Completely alone, like Lola. I'm not going to have *anybody*. Who cares about an old woman. I'm going to get old and I'm not ... I'm ... Nobody's going to take care of me ..." She starts to cry full out, so I pull up closer to her on the bed and put my hand on her shoulder. "Honey, you're a tenured professor, you go to conferences all over the world. You make a hundred thousand dollars a year." I'm trying to be reasonable but all it does is make her sob louder. I'm getting desperate. I can't stand it when she cries. "Look, don't worry. *I'll* take care of you."

She rolls over and looks at me.

"*You*? You! All *you* are going to do is keep drinking and smoking so much you'll be dead in the next ten years, and the whole while you'll be chasing younger and younger women around in a pathetic attempt to crawl into bed with them. *You*, that's what you'll do!"

She's got a point but it puts me on the defensive anyway. I'm thinking I'll get up and go into my own room. She's got her room, I've got mine. We're not stupid.

"You want me to stay?"

She sniffles but doesn't say anything. It's like she's weighing the options. Finally she whispers, "No ..."

That's what she says, no, very quietly. Only the thing is, I know her, and what she really means is "Yes."

So I stay and she's sobbing a little softer. I'm trying to think of what to say to her to make her feel better, only I'm not very good at it.

I just lie there scratching her back, the way she likes it.

Stash

FOR WHAT IT'S worth, I have five brothers; none of them are close to me. Jacob manages a pizza outlet and is facing jail time for punching a fourteen-year-old hockey referee in the mouth. He barely speaks to his wife, hates his job, and is convinced his eleven-year-old son is about to get drafted and become a millionaire hockey player.

Allan is forty-six and closest to me in age. He's fond of board games but intolerant of lactose and public housing. His wife is a belly dancer with an eating disorder; a problem which, according to Allan, is epidemic in the belly dancing profession.

Jeremy is the youngest of the family and the black sheep. Two years ago he stole a wedge of brie from a supermarket in Penticton, British Columbia and spent three days in jail for it.

Mortimer is fifty-three and has fathered two overweight children. He buys and sells stocks on the Internet and has more money than he knows what to do with. Nicky, his twin, is an accountant and is undergoing what he calls a hydrotherapy program in an attempt to cure a chocolate addiction.

You might say that my family has issues around food.

My father, who died a month ago, ate like a horse. Even confined to hospital he ate like a horse. On my last visit I found him lying on his cot, grey, skinny, and wolfing down a tray full of potatoes and carrots.

"Shelly," he gulped. "There's something I want you to do for me."

"Sure, just go ahead and tell me, Dad."

"There's a few things at the house. You know, a few ... a few ... magazines."

"Magazines?"

"They're not really magazines. I mean, there's some magazines. They're more like movies. You get me? Videos."

"Overdue videos? You want me to take them back?"

"They're not really overdue, Shell. I mean, they're not even mine." He was squirming now. "They're somebody else's. A buddy, from the war."

"Dad," I said softly, "you weren't in the war."

My father bolted upright. "I was so! The *Korean* War. I was a cook. I want you to dispose of them."

"Pardon me?"

"Get rid of them. Burn them. Throw them out. I don't give a damn, Shell, just get rid of them. I don't want your mother seeing them, that's all. She's had enough with me, hasn't she? They're in a plastic bag in the tool shed."

I understood then what he wanted.

On my way out of the hospital I met my mother sailing down the hall, clutching a large silver bag containing a cooked chicken. The ward was beginning to smell like a rotisserie takeout joint.

"Shell, how is he? Is he ... is he ... hungry?"

"Sure, he's hungry."

"Oh good." She squeezed my shoulder and swept by me.

I FOUND DAD'S collection of smut wrapped in a white plastic grocery bag in what, for some reason, we have always called his tool shed, even though the only tool my father knew how to operate was a bottle opener. The bag was stashed beneath an overturned barbecue and an empty golf bag. I took it and drove home feeling bad. All my life I've carried my father's physical traits with me; his jawline, his splayed feet, his long nose and expansive forehead. I've lugged around his interest in food, his nervousness, and the assumption that at any moment I was likely to fall into a coma or get clobbered by a brick thrown from a bridge. And now I was carting about his pornography.

The bag sat beside me like a severed head, stuffed with forty years of anxiety. I was tempted to roll down the window and heave the thing into traffic, or chuck it onto the parkway. I had a vision of soiled back issues of *Spread Eagle* fluttering up and down the valley like pigeon feathers. Instead I parked at a grade school near a bridge and slunk into the shadows. Far to my left the Parkway surged like lava, and beneath me I saw the earth cut with chalk-coloured bicycle paths. I lifted the package and was about to let it go into an overstuffed public garbage bin, but for some reason I could not let go. I heard the grunts and groans of orgasmic porn stars coming from inside the bag, their lives continuously fast-forwarded to the good parts, and for some reason I could not do it.

I went back to the car, and slapped *Ranch of the Nymphomaniac Girls* and *Massive Boobs in Motion Vol. II* on the seat beside me and drove directly to the Kew Garden Café. At the Kew Garden I'm known as the woman who writes a column for *Wine and Dine*. Perhaps I'm also known as the woman who slept with the chef, a drug-addled Paraguayan named Carlos whose specialty is boiled beef *matelote à la Bourgeoise*. I ordered the *pissaladière* instead and found it slightly too literal. Later, the squash-blossom *beignets* reminded me of why I had slept with that cokehead in the first place.

IN THE MORNING I woke up and heard the garbage truck clanging and grinding from the curb. I had just enough time to jump into my fuzzy bear slippers, wrap my housecoat around myself, and offer Dad's porno to the nice garbage men proceeding up the street. Instead, the telephone rang.

"Shelly?"

It was Jennifer, Allan's wife. She pities me because I don't belly dance and I'm not married.

"Yes?"

"Whatever differences you've had with your father Shelley, you better put them aside."

"What differences?" I said.

"Let's not talk about that now, Shelly. That's something for you and your therapist to resolve. Allan just called from the hospital; your father's dying."

I hung up the phone, drove to the hospital, and arrived two minutes too late. Allan was there with a doctor and a nurse. A half-eaten baloney sandwich had fallen from Dad's fingers and lay on the floor, mustard-side down.

THE FUNERAL TOOK place in a freak May snowstorm. By then none of my brothers were speaking to each other. Three of them had retained lawyers. The bank had put a lien on my father's two cars and a skip tracer was harassing my mother. The eulogy was spoken by a skinny Presbyterian minister who wore a ponytail, and during the course of it, Mortimer's children played hand-held video games. When it was over I went home and ate every chocolate truffle I could lay my hands on.

The following day, in the rain, I took my father's pornography and drove to Mortimer's. I anticipated that Mortimer would come to the door holding the business section of the newspaper in one hand and a radio-phone in the other. Before he could apologize for being too busy to invite me in, I'd ram the package into his belly — "This belonged to *your* father. Here, he wanted *you* to have it."

Instead I was met at the door by Mortimer's two children, both of them dressed in combat fatigues and heavily armed with ray guns.

"Dad's busy."

Mortimer's voice cut in irritably from the living room, "Who is it?"

"It's an alien," answered one kid, his finger already twitching on the trigger.

"Yeah, it's an alien," chimed the brother. "Blast her! Fry the alien!"

I fled before they could achieve this.

Next I drove to Jacob's. His house was modest and seemed to crouch in fear behind a maple tree. The tree had been hit by lightning. Jacob wasn't home, I knew that. Today was his arraignment. For a moment I imagined my brother on the stand, ferocious and indignant: "It was in the net, your Honour. The puck was clearly *in* the net!" I would've driven to Allan's too but he'd recently taken his family and moved them deep into the suburbs, away from the lactose and public housing. So I drove to Nicky's instead, and rang the doorbell three times. Nicky came to the door in a frayed bathrobe and was clearly in a relapse. His lips, his mouth, even his earlobes, were smeared with chocolate.

"Jesus, Shell. Look at me!"

"I can't talk now," I said, wildly, and ran back to the car with my father's bag-o-porn slapping against my knee.

I drove to Jeremy's next. Jeremy, for some reason, was hiding behind the door. As soon as I knocked it flew open and there he was, naked from the waist up, holding a dumbbell in his right hand and sporting a new tattoo.

"Hey sis," he said. "Want to puff a doobie?"

I left my brother's house stoned, still clutching Dad's porno, and starving for macaroons and lemon gelato. Halfway to my mother's house I pulled into a donut shop for six plain, uncomplicated donuts, and ate them in the car.

When I turned into my mother's driveway I saw a light shining from the kitchen. The living room was dark and it felt like it would stay that way for a long time. I'd eaten shortbread cookies in that room. For fifteen years my brothers had teased, tormented, and body-slammed me on the thick broadloom of that floor. My hamster had died beneath the sofa in there after chewing a plastic bread tab. My father, following a disagreement over who exactly had scored the overtime winner in a 1965 Stanley Cup game, had heaved the Christmas turkey through the same bay window that was dark and curtained now.

Mom came to the door, ruddy with tears. Her face was pink and swollen and marked with shards of crucified makeup.

"Hello, dear," she said gamely. "I didn't know you were coming. I would have cooked something."

I shut the door behind me and followed her into the kitchen. A pizza box sat on the table, and the refrigerator thrummed sadly in the corner. All my life it has done that.

"Mom," I said. "I've got something for you. It's from Dad."

"From your father?"

"Yes, it's from Dad."

I handed her the bag which she placed on the table next to the pizza box and opened gingerly, hopefully, as if expecting a genie to come steaming through the top. Nothing like that happened, so she reached inside and came out with a videotape instead. She put her reading glasses on.

"*Ranch of the Nymphomaniac Girls*," she recited carefully, pronouncing every syllable. Her arm vanished into the bag and came out with *Massive Boobs in Motion Vol. II*. She didn't say anything this time. Finally she retrieved the magazines and dropped them back into the bag.

"It's porno. It's Dad's porno."

She looked at me.

"He wanted you to have it."

She removed her glasses and rubbed her left eye with the back of her wrist. "Me? He said that?"

"I don't know," I said. "I'm sorry."

"Your father." She tried to laugh. "I ... Really ... I ..." Then she was crying. "Oh, Shell, what am I going to do? I miss that son of a bitch so much."

I was crying too. I leaned over and put my arms around her.

"Mom," I sobbed, "*oh*, Mom."

Life Without Death

FOR SEVERAL MONTHS Frank Cole shared an apartment with a young woman I had fallen in love with. We met each other in that apartment enough times for him not to like me. Both of us were twenty-one years old, opinionated, argumentative, and we fought about poetry in particular. We sat at a kitchen table in a second floor apartment on Elgin Street in downtown Ottawa and fought about poetry. Sara, the woman I was in love with, was radiant and barefoot, her legs on the table, the coffee dripping through a filter, and the fragrance of cigarette smoke filling the room. Frank was an intense young man, with large eyes that were not unfriendly, and a large and bulging forehead that indicated, at least to me, that he possessed too much intelligence; the kind of intelligence that in the end is perhaps not useful to anyone. That intense head already showed a widow's peak, and I consoled myself in the belief that Frank would go bald before me. At that age I could imagine no greater catastrophe than to lose my hair.

Out the window of that apartment I watched a girls' base-ball game unwinding on lush grass next to a high school, and inside I watched Sara go about her activities in the kitchen. I have pictures of that time; it is hard to believe that she could be so young, that her hair could be so thick, or that she, anyone, could be so lovely. Poetry was on the table and the smell of oil paint and pastels hung in the apartment. Frank was clicking a camera. Apparently he was a photographer. I paid little attention. Everyone, it seemed to me, was a photographer back then. I, of course, was not a photographer; I was a poet. The only profession that mattered.

Frank had put on the table three poems written by a fifteen-year-old girl; his niece, I believe. He was extremely impressed by them and wanted me to be impressed too. I read them but I was not impressed at all. I told Frank that they were the sort of poems I would expect a fifteen-year-old girl to write. This angered him and he told me, angrily, that I was wrong. I didn't care what he thought. I was a poet; I thought it was my duty to anger people. In the end things smoothed themselves out. Sara told me that Frank had reappraised the poems, and come to the conclusion that they were not as brilliant as he first thought. I did not see this as a victory. Looking back now, I think this exchange revealed something about Frank Cole: a generosity toward others, a willingness to forgive, and an understanding about the futility of getting angry with people.

Three years passed before I encountered Frank again. I had moved to Toronto, and entered into the underground world of poetry which to me meant living in a succession of Toronto garrets and basements where mice left paw prints in the frying pan, and cockroaches disappeared behind counters the moment you switched the lights on. Sara was dead, murdered, is how I put it, by a drunken boater, a neurosurgeon, who collided his powerboat into her while she was out swimming in a lake in northern Quebec. She was wearing a blue bathing suit when she was killed and I convinced myself I had bought this suit for her as a gift for her twenty-third birthday, although now after so many years, I don't think I did.

At the time she was killed she was painting sets for a Canadian feature film called *Blue Boy*, a biopic about Canadian rower Ned Hanlan. Hanlan's Point on the Toronto Islands is named after him. The film is dedicated to her. "Too bad," said a mutual friend, "that the film wasn't any good." Today this remark strikes me as well-intentioned, but strange, implying as it does that if the film had been better, then somehow, her death would have been less meaningless.

During this time I took menial jobs largely because I thought this is what writers did, poets in particular, but also because I lacked the confidence to compete for anything else. I put beer in the fridges of the Edgewater Hotel and watched one morning as the paramedics wheeled out a body, the right hand extended stiffly straight up in the air. I unloaded grain from the freighters that moored alongside the silos of the mills, and between shifts I walked to the café at Harbourfront for lunch, or to kill time. It was while walking the long sterile halls of that establishment that I saw an exhibition of photos by Frank Cole mounted on the corridor walls.

I was not pleased to see them. They made me feel that I had fallen behind, that as I stood waist deep in a brown sea of soybeans downbound from Thunder Bay, I was not furthering my art in any way that I had presumed I was. The photographs were black and white, and each one of them depicted a very old person in the first stages of death, or the very last stage of life.

They were cold, grim, unrelenting, and they recorded in stark detail the hospital death of a very elderly person, a grandparent who was no more than a parchment of grey skin stretched across brittle bones. Frank was fascinated with old age, with the decay and the sickness of it, and his photographs demonstrated this. I rejected them right there on the spot. I rejected them because I was young, I rejected their elitist presentation. I rejected the focus, but I was troubled by the extremity of their formal power. I went back to my miserable job unloading grain from grain boats and did not think much about it anymore.

I WOULD NOT encounter Frank Cole again for twenty-five years. In that time I had my life. I wrote books, I painted paintings, I canoed rivers, I hit the road. I fell in and out of love with a succession of remarkable women, I lost a fair amount of my hair. Then, for reasons not clear to me, I became the father of two small girls and my life, as I knew it, disappeared. Instead of reading Kadare novels in translation from the Albanian, I washed dishes and folded laundry and when that was done I made peanut butter sandwiches and cooked, and then I folded laundry and washed dishes. If I wrote at all, I did so with my youngest daughter's legs wrapped around my neck and my older daughter singing from beneath my desk. I read *The Berenstain Bears* until I couldn't stand it anymore.

I no longer believed that writing would make the world right, not even *my* writing. Then, one night, having read *The Berenstain Bears* and *The Rainbow Goblins* and put my children mercifully to bed, I lay flat out on the sofa, scrolling the television in an exhausted haze. I began to watch something about the Sahara Desert. Everything was in black and white, grim, grainy, and depressing — yet familiar. I watched, and I realized very quickly that I was watching footage taken by Frank Cole, even footage *of* Frank Cole. I watched, mesmerized by what was in front of me; there was Frank, twenty-five years on, his widow's peak stubbornly intact. There he was in the desert, filming his own body as it fell apart in the heat. There he was pulling a growth off the nose of a camel. There were the frenetic insects of the sand, devouring each other, the bones of the dead animals that stuck out of the desert like the ribs of ships. All of this was intercut with images of Frank's grandfather dying of old age in a hospital. I had seen these photographs before on the walls of Harbourfront twenty-five years ago.

The film was titled *Life Without Death*, and it was the sort of masterpiece that comes of a talented artist following an idea to the very end. I lay on the sofa and watched. I thought of me and Frank and Sara in that kitchen thirty years ago and our silly little spat over poetry, and for a moment I felt sick with the belief that I could have done something, I could have said something back then to stop this thing that was waiting to happen. "Frank," I would say to him, "sometimes what we believe in, what we know to be right, will take us to places that are very far away, dangerous places. You need to be careful Frank, we all need to be careful." And I would look over at Sara, barefoot, and I would warn her too.

FRANK COLE HAD done something that no one else had ever done before, something that, weirdly enough, had secured him an entry into *The Guinness Book of World Records*. Twenty years after our little spat in that Ottawa apartment he set out to cross the Sahara Desert alone, on a camel, from Néma,

Mauritania, to the coast of the Red Sea in Sudan, a distance of some seven thousand kilometres. I am speculating about the distance because no one really knows how far it is from Néma, Mauritania to the Sudanese coast of the Red Sea. No one has ever done it except Frank, and he did it lugging three Bolex 16-millimetre cameras and a tripod in a pre-digital age when every piece of equipment was heavy; even the tins that contained Frank's film were heavy. At times he trusted himself to guides, even though they were sometimes not trustworthy at all — some were, in fact, criminals. He got lost. There were times when he realized that even his guides were lost. At one point he was lost for six weeks. Saharan authorities threw him into jail, more than once. They did not know what to make of this strange foreigner who had no fear of the desert or of bandits, and more likely than not were trying to save his life by putting him in jail. In the end Frank wore them down with his tenacity, writing letters to any embassy he could, demanding, begging to be allowed out of his cell so he could go on with his project. In the film an exasperated police officer demands of him, "Don't you care about death?"

"How could he know," says Frank to the camera in a slow and disturbing voice, "that death was all I cared about?"

I understood then Frank's fascination with the ancient and the dying, at least I think I did. I understood those photographs, I understood this astonishing film called *Life Without Death*. I was sitting upright by this point, shocked, and realized that Frank had set out to formally solve death. Frank had seen a way through it. Death was a problem, and it could be solved. But first it was necessary to train for it, and he did; he trained for months by lifting weights, I saw him in the film lifting those weights, I saw his excruciatingly strict regime of vitamins, the rigorous exclusion of fat, *any* fat, from his diet, I saw his bare Ottawa apartment as he rid himself of all physical objects, finally breaking off any human contact whatsoever. He was ready to defeat death.

AFTER HE RETURNED from the desert, Frank Cole spent the following ten years editing his film. It premiered in Paris. Then, when he was done with that, he returned to the Sahara Desert to do his trip all over again. This time he would cross the Sahara from the Atlantic Ocean to the Red Sea, but once he reached the Red Sea he would turn around and go back, and he would do it all over again in reverse.

He set out on October 19, 2000. A few days later, his bludgeoned body was found tied to a tree outside of Timbuktu. I found this a strange detail, that the body of a dead man would be tied to a tree, and I began to wonder why the bandits who had murdered Frank found it necessary to do this. Then I knew, I knew with shocking clarity, for Frank had solved death, he was not joking about this, it was not something he was doing for some artistic reason. It was real. He had achieved life without death. Even with his skull bashed in, he would not give up; he rose repeatedly from the sand and in a civil and firm voice demanded that his assassins return his Bolex cameras and film canisters. They had no choice but to tie his restless and dead body to a tree.

Frank's film was followed by a short documentary on his life and while it was going on my five-year-old came down from her bedroom and stood on the stairs clutching a blanket.

"Daddy, I had a bad dream."

This was a ruse, I knew it; she knew that I knew it, but usually it worked. "Come here then," I said and she flew down the stairs and leapt onto the sofa with me.

The documentary closed with a long shot of Frank Cole, staring at the camera; the smiling, intelligent face of a man who knew many things, perhaps too many.

"Is that man dead?" My daughter was five, but she knew, or sensed already, that to be in a photograph often meant that you were dead. The world is full of pictures of people who are dead.

"Yes," I said, "he is."

"Was he your friend?"

I looked at her, I saw her eyes, and I saw that they were not brown but amber and that they were even more beautiful than I remembered from several hours before.

"No, sweetheart, not a friend. He was just someone I knew a long time ago."

The World in the Evening

THE PHONE RINGS and I'm told matter-of-factly that Ray Bowlen suffered a seizure on a beach in Waikiki, fell into a coma, and was pronounced dead on Tuesday of last week. Moments tick off and I sense these moments require something from me; a vision of my own death, the death of my wife, and even my daughter who is not yet six. Instead I have a sudden, heartbreaking memory of my cat who threw a blood clot a month ago, and died in agony on a steel table while an incompetent vet with wine on his breath tried to stick a needle into her paw.

With the phone pressed to my ear I remember not Ray Bowlen, but the book I borrowed from him a long time ago; a first printing of *The World in the Evening* by Christopher Isherwood. The dust jacket is immaculate and the title page signed by the author. I remember his looping signature inscribed at a boozy publishing function in New York, where Ray Bowlen and, for that matter, Mr. Isherwood were both drinking themselves to death.

But suddenly Ray is dead, and all that comes to my mind is a book I borrowed from him and forgot to return, as if one led to the other. Finally I manage, "Oh no," but this doesn't seem right either, not for Ray, who by the age of twelve was what he called "a ditch drunk," and at seventeen lived on skid row in New Orleans where he slept with a knife in one hand, and a shampoo bottle filled with methylated spirits in the other. "Oh no" will not do for that vigorous, elderly man who made his way about the city on an artificial hip and two knees make out of tungsten.

No sooner have I said "Oh no" than the signed copy of *The World in the Evening* stands out from my book shelf. By now it's the largest book I own; larger than the World Atlas. Even the King James Bible is dwarfed by this book. I see myself sitting down at one of the coffee places that Ray frequented, eating chocolate-covered biscotti. I pass his book back to him across the table and he says, "Oh thank you," only he says it with such warmth that I feel I've done the man a huge favour. That was Ray; he spent forty years of his life a desperate alcoholic. He collapsed on the street with such frequency that ambulance drivers came to know him by his first name. More than once he packed his cat into a suitcase in the belief that both he and it were flying first class to Vancouver. Then, after his second grand mal seizure, he was touched by the gods and got clean. After that if you walked through the same room that Ray was in you felt better for it.

WHEN MY FATHER passed away I knew even less than I do now about death and how we are supposed to behave around it. I stood in a dim hospital room and what I realized then was that when men died they often died in the presence of women. They died in front of their wives and daughters, or their girlfriends and mistresses; the same women they had taken for granted for so many years and now were utterly dependent on. They died in front of young nurses who wore flat shoes and meant well but talked to grown men as though they were little boys. "How we doing today, tiger?" "Don't you worry, sonny, we'll have you back in that little room of yours in a jiffy."

That's how they talked to my father when the mask of death was on his face and they had him dressed in a blue hospital gown that didn't cover his buttocks. I was furious with them. What did they know about this gigantic, dying man who had defended their country in Tripoli and Kasserine, and had once joked and shared a cigarette with a nineteen-year-old boy from Goderich, Ontario, moments before his body was snapped apart by a tank shell?

I was angry with those nurses, but really I was angry with my old man. He was a decent father; game to pick up a baseball glove or a hockey stick, but he was a lousy husband and I remembered the hollering that seeped through the dark rooms of being a kid and I was furious with the poor man. He was dying and I couldn't stand it. I couldn't stand *him*, I couldn't stand that he was dying, and I could not stand the way the nurses talked to him. Stop it! I wanted to shout. This man is eighty-eight years old and he fought at Kasserine and he fought for freedom which is more than *you* will *ever* do, and he does not need to be talked to like a child. In the end I kept my mouth shut. I'm glad I did.

RAY BOWLEN DID not die like my father. His life did not end in a dim hospital room where he was separated by a curtain from another man who, I'm sure, had been dead for some time. The only indication he was not dead came twice a day when a group of elderly women entered the room and said, "How are you feeling today, George?" When the form on the bed didn't respond they whispered, "Oh, he's so tired," and pulled the hospital sheets up to his face, which was already the colour of ash.

Ray did not die in a room that had no paintings hanging from the wall or Greek nudes taped to the fridge, cat hair on the carpet, or Belgian chocolates in ornate golden wrappers cached about the place in case of emergencies. Ray died on a beach in Waikiki, smeared in suntan lotion, in the company of young men who were also smeared in suntan lotion.

I saw him for the last time at a Thanksgiving dinner. He sat in a chair with his crutches propped against the wall and a young man sitting in his lap. Ray was seventy-two years old, the top buttons of his shirt were undone, a garland of plastic flowers adorned his head, and the young man was apparently trying to remove something from Ray's ear with his tongue. He looked the way I imagine Cicero might have looked; old, lecherous and very alive.

My wife and I were leaving when Ray spotted us. He craned his neck to one side, indicated somehow that we were at least as important to him as the young man parked on his knees. "Thank you so much for the ride," he said cheerfully. Every Thanksgiving we drove him from his apartment to dinner and his appreciation was so genuine that it shocked us. My wife and I were having troubles then, but we drove home without either of us being disappointed in the other. "He's wonderful," she said. Something of Ray Bowlen had passed into us, and we were better for it.

FOR THE TIME being I have taken in Ray's cat. It sits in a corner of the house near the radiator wilfully missing the litter box and glaring at me. I also went through Ray's papers, putting his bills and estate matters in a neat pile and shredding the rest. Ray Bowlen's occupation had always been mysterious to me, and maybe even to him, It had to do with the writing of reports, and was governmental in nature, although one summer Ray was somehow involved in the trial of a Toronto police officer who had done something to a sixteen-year-old girl in the back seat of his cruiser. It seems Ray took complicated issues and made them simple for a living.

He lived in a high-rise apartment in a modest junior one bedroom. His bookshelves contained a hardcover copy of Richard Fariña's book, books by Thomas Wolfe, books that were often intimately signed; coffee table books showing muscular men in white bathing trunks stretched on the decks of yachts. It seems Ray had a thing about yachts or at least muscular men in white bathing trunks who splayed their bodies on the decks of them. He had a fondness for sentimental recovery books written in a sugary greeting-card style. His personal correspondence was voluminous and erratic; a thank-you note from the Neighbourhood Committee on Pet Microchipping, a complex, three-page explanation from a public health officer on the role of digoxin in the treatment of childhood heart disease. This errata forms the book of anyone's life, but the book I was looking for was the book about Ray Bowlen.

It was long assumed by people who knew him that Ray was writing his autobiography. I was hoping to finding this manuscript on the hard drive of his computer or behind Ray's bookshelf or beneath his mattress — any of the places a man conceals the draft of the novel he intends to write, or the pornographic magazines he one day intends to throw out.

I had great hopes for it, already mapping out a few chapters in my mind. I imagined it beginning in the suburbs of Vancouver with fat skunks waddling in the rain from one garbage can to the next. From there the scene would move to the pumphouse behind the sewage plant: a boy treated to wine and a quarter hour of incomprehensible fondling. It lurched blackout by blackout into Ray's boozy teens and arrived, like Ray himself, in New York where, against all odds, he became a successful sales rep for Random House, and one of many young men who came to New York, drank too much, and ended up sleeping with Christopher Isherwood. Then to Toronto where Ray became what he called a leather boy, riding about on a little motor scooter wearing denim jeans, a black leather jacket, and a white T-shirt — the costume of his queerness when there wasn't even a word for it. He had known men who took him home one night and blackmailed him the next. He knew what it took to square your shoulders and walk directly into the St. Charles Tavern.

It was also said about Ray that as a young man he'd had a relationship with a professional hockey player who was prone to getting drunk and beating up his boyfriends. One night he put Ray in the hospital with a broken cheekbone and three cracked ribs. Following that his friends hid him in their apartments whenever the player's team showed up in town. Apparently, after the game, the man scoured the city in a cab gulping from a bottle of Canadian Club, and looking for Ray Bowlen. Under no circumstance would Ray give up his identity. "He was extremely famous," said Ray, scandalized at the very thought of outing him. "I don't think the country could stand it."

That was something I admired about Ray; he didn't kiss and tell. He was a patriot. He wasn't a writer. I never found a manuscript.

WHEN MY FATHER died he was frightened of the pain that came to him at night. It was the type of pain that could be counted on, and it clutched at his chest like the talons of a hawk. When he was not frightened he was angry at death for daring to enter his room. He was angry at old lance corporals and generals, and mostly he was furious that death had crept into his life and was about to take control of it.

There were times when he tried to express this to me. His neck drew in and out like a canvas tent as he fought for the words. "It's like ... it's like a knife." His voice was bitter, exasperated, and he made a fast sweeping gesture with his arm, turning it into a scythe that was shearing him off at the legs. "The worst is I can't tell you, I can't describe it." He clenched his fists. I saw for the last time the long, talented fingers that had held grand slams on legendary bridge nights. Those evenings are gone now, like TV dinners and nuclear fallout shelters. I saw hands that had once curled a perfect eight-ender; the same hands that fastened together the custom-built two-piece pool cue my father insisted had paid his way through college. I was looking at hands that had tousled the hair of children, though I do not remember him doing that with me. Those hands had passed rugby footballs to his mates, shoved pointed shells into the breeches of tank cannons; fumbled with blouses and garters and removed elaborate lingerie from the bodies of beautiful women. I looked at those hands and they shocked me; a child's rusted Meccano set, worn out, with the cables frayed and pieces missing. A thin wrist with the veins showing, vanished into the sleeve of his hospital gown. The doctors had taken blood from his finger and I knew this procedure had been extraordinarily painful; the sort of thing my father would love to tell later in the hope of making people laugh.

All his life my father had been a sportsman and now he was losing the game and that made him furious. The pain frightened him. I didn't know what to say to this man as he died. I didn't know how to look at him. In a crazy moment I thought he would rise up from his bed and protect me from death, that he would protect all of us. That's what I thought on the night he died. I was about to start smoking again and I thought of his anger and the broken dishes, even the broken houses that he had left behind him, and somewhere, while I was thinking that, his life ended.

I WENT OUTSIDE into the dark. The catalpa trees were in thick bloom and for some reason the smell made me think of my mother. She was nineteen years old on a troop train pounding over the Shield on her way to Kenora, Ontario. The train had stopped to coal and all the young soldiers went out and picked wildflowers for her. The steward arranged an entire car with them; black-eyed Susans, yarrow, evening primrose and wild phlox. Four hundred young men in uniform had fallen in love with my nineteen-year-old mother. Across the north shore of Lake Superior they came in rotating groups down the aisle, presenting her flowers and fighting for the right to sing to her. "They were all singing to me," she laughed. "It was the time of my life."

For a moment her face came to me then was gone. In the light of the hospital lobby I saw a man at the payphone explaining to someone far away that the world was darker now than before.

The Fight

ON THE EVENING of the fight, Gordy Davenport was waiting for me at the bottom of the street by the Yates's place where the creek ran underneath the street. It was seven o'clock and I was supposed to be at the football field at seven thirty because that's where the fight was. This was an official fight with dates, times, witnesses, and everything. What, exactly, it was about, I wasn't sure anymore. All I knew was that we were playing touch football at school, Steve Bodegan pushed me, so I pushed him back and Bodegan said, "Oh yeah?" and I said, "Oh yeah?" and after that there was no stopping the thing.

Gordy was there leaning on the little bridge by the creek and he picked up alongside me without talking. We went in a hurry past the Keegstra place because Polly Keegstra was a big stupid kid and at any moment he could come flying out of his house and beat you up for no reason. Then we got to the maple tree in front of the cemetery and I slowed down to look up in the branches to see if Pete Moffat was up there. Pete's dad was a boozer, so Pete spent a lot of his free time up in that tree, sitting up there on a branch with a bucket filled with water that he'd lugged up there with him. When a girl walked by that he had a thing for, he poured the water on her head.

I heard some rustling in the branches, and then Pete dropped straight down, feet-first to the sidewalk, like someone whose parachute hadn't opened properly.

"You goin' to fight Bodegan?"

"Yeah, I am."

"He's fast, right. You got to watch for that."

"I know he's fast."

"But you're fast too, right?"

"Right," I said.

"Only he's *really* fast. So don't let him get close to you, 'cause if he gets too close you won't even see him. He'll murdle-ize you. What you got to do is like this." Pete made a few gestures as if he was dancing with a fat lady. "Stevie Bodegan high-jumped five foot seven at a track meet in Cayuga, you know."

"Yeah, I know that."

"That's a record."

"Yeah," I said, "I know that."

WE TOOK THE shortcut through the cemetery, like we always did on the way to school, stopping halfway up the hill at the monument to the Unknown Soldier where the flag flew on a tall white pole.

"You know what this is for," said Gordy, kicking at the flagstones. "It's for all those guys who had their heads shot off in the war. Guys whose faces were blown right off. So you can't tell who they are anymore. They stick them in here. What's left of them."

I nodded but I didn't say anything because I didn't believe it. I knew from my father, who had fought, that it was just a

monument, a white brick wall with a bronze plaque and a flag-
pole sticking up to commemorate all the men who died in the
war and never came back, whether their faces were blown off
or not. They were still over there. They were unknown.

We trudged on up the terraced hills, stopping, as we always
did, at the gravestone with the glass case in it. Behind that glass
was the grey steel vase inscribed with words and filled with
ashes. We stood silently in front of it, seeing our faces reflected
in the glass. Gordy read out loud, "'By their Labour shall ye
know them.' Weird," he said.

It was weird, and I had no desire to be staring at a guy
whose body had been burnt down into to a heap of ashes and
put in a jar. It reminded me of the ashtrays that marked my
mother's passage in the house. "Let's get out of here," I said.

The two of us walked on without talking until we reached
the water tap. Even though my mouth was dry as wood, I refused
to drink from it. I waited for Gordy, who turned his mouth
beneath the tap and took a long, slurping swallow. It was just
something that he did whether he was thirsty or not.

By now it was getting dark and the shadows extended from
the bases of the gravestones, reaching across the grass and just
lying there like some person who had passed out. A few bats
whipped around in the dusk. I was scared. I felt it. Of course
I was scared; Steve Bodegan was thirteen years old, the most
dangerous age for a boy to be, especially if you had to fight him.
No one in living memory had ever won a fight against Steve
Bodegan. There were perplexing rumours about Steve Bodegan
that boys told with awe. Stories that involved girls. Sometimes
Bodegan carried around a two-piece pool cue in a black case.
The family was big, *too* big, indecently big, and they lived in

a wartime house down by the creek with a front yard that had cars on it that didn't work, old refrigerators that didn't work either, and a chained-up dog that barked all the time.

In case all of this wasn't bad enough, Bodegan was also close friends with Al Southall and Maxie Dunnigan, who were older and knew more swear words than any other kid in town. They had already got drunk on homemade wine and famously puked behind the bandshell. They had also taken sleeping bags to Lake Huron and hung out with American guys who wore beads around their necks and refused to go to Vietnam, coming back from these visits with marijuana and little plastic bags with pills in them. There was no way in the world that I was going to beat Steve Bodegan in a fight. I was just a twelve-year-old kid who hadn't even taken drugs or done things to girls.

We reached the end of the cemetery and marched down the concrete steps to the park where the football field was. By now Gordy was punching one hand into the palm of the other, like he was my trainer, or something. I wished he would stop doing that. The park was empty, at least the tennis courts were empty, and dark except for a few streetlights. A car with one working headlight crept around like a Cyclops, finally gunned its engine, and roared away. Halfway across the park the lights from the lawn-bowling pitch burned bright white over top of the old people dressed in white, and bent like sticks.

We passed the overgrown field filled with timothy and gold-enrod in front of Mike Aldershot's house. Mike had been taken out of school because a hockey puck struck him in the face and took out five of his teeth. Since then he ate everything through a straw. Then we came to the spot where I saw a deer one morning on the way to school, a small one, bolting out of the grass in front of the hill, but no one believed me. No one had ever seen a deer there before. Gordy pointed to a spot higher up.

"Remember that place?"

Sure I did. Last year, walking to school together, we saw two men lying in the high grass with their arms around each other. Later, after school, we told Gordy's brother about it. "When men do that," he'd explained to us, "it's called 'being a homo' and you got to get out of there real fast."

We passed the high school and the spot by the telephone pole where one of the students had killed himself with his dad's shotgun during the Sadie Hawkins dance. Everyone said it was because the guy was in love with a girl who broke it off with him. The next day the workers came and spread sand across the grass so me and Gordy couldn't see the blood anymore.

At last we got to the football field and I looked around expecting to see Al Southall and Maxie Dunnigan. All day I had imagined them waiting for me with their arms folded and Steve Bodegan standing in front, opening and shutting a jackknife. But there was no one around, and it was too dark to see the goalposts at the other end of the field.

"Maybe he's down at the other end," said Gordy.

We walked and each time we got to a ten-yard hash mark, Gordy gave it a kick and a puff of lime dust sprayed up and dusted the turf.

I stopped. "You hear that?"

"What?"

"That."

"I didn't hear nothing."

"Hear it?"

Somewhere at the other end of the park the last bit of laughter, or a scream, melted away into the night and was replaced by the barking of a dog. "I thought I heard something."

"Probably just someone screaming," said Gordy.

"Yeah," I said, and nodded. For reasons I had never been able to fathom, people were always screaming at night. When I lay in bed I heard them pealing out of the dark; weird screams that came out of nowhere and were gone in a second. Sometimes I thought the whole night was filled with screams, the entire world. Sometimes I thought I heard the thrilling wild voices of girls, like curls of smoke coming out of chimneys on winter nights; high-pitched sounds. I thought maybe these screams were what older kids did when they began to grow up, although it was not impossible someone was really getting murdered out there in the dark, like Sandra Danzinger, who was stabbed and thrown off a balcony.

"I don't see him."

"Yeah, maybe he's not coming."

I looked at him.

"What do you mean?"

"Maybe he's not coming."

"Not coming?" Sometimes Gordy could say stupid things.

"Yeah, watch." He put both his hands to his mouth and hollered, "Hey, Bodegan!" The words echoed three times against the escarpment and fell away into the dark.

Somewhere far off I heard the tail end of someone screaming, or laughing, or getting murdered, and then nothing. Just the dark.

"See," said Gordy. "He ain't coming. He's probably doing it with someone. He's probably doing it with Penny Blandin."

"He is not," I answered grimly. Only a month ago Penny

Blandin had let me kiss her behind the pickup truck that sat on the bricks in her backyard. I remembered the peck of my flesh against her flesh. Our teeth had clanged for a moment.

Gordy looked at me and then looked away. "I don't know," he said. "But he ain't here."

"Yeah," I agreed. "He ain't here."

"He didn't show," said Gordy. "So you win. Those are the rules."

AND IN FACT those *were* the rules. Steve Bodegan wasn't there. He was supposed to be there, and he wasn't. For a moment I felt good about myself and my circumstances, I felt expansive and generous like I wanted to give Gordy some money or something, and then after that I just felt stupid. Stevie Bodegan was out driving a girl around on his bike. Of course that's what he was doing. I saw Penny Blandin on the handlebars of Bodegan's bike; laughing, her hair flying back and getting in Bodegan's face and tickling him. And I felt more than a stab of envy, I felt a hatchet chop of it, right in the chest.

But still, Stevie Bodegan wasn't there. And *I* was. This meant something to me. It had to mean something. It meant I was not a coward.

"You know what?" I said.

"What?"

"You have to do what you're supposed to do. Like, what's right. As long as you do that, things'll work out good for you."

Gordy thought about that. "What do you mean? Like, if you do what you're supposed to do, you'll end up in heaven or something?"

"Yeah," I said. "You'll end up in heaven. Or something like that."

"You think so?"

"I don't know. Maybe."

"Yeah," said Gordy. "Who knows?"

And together we turned around and started back toward the path that led through the cemetery.